TAKING A CHANCE 1

TAKING A CHANCE

REED AND RICE SERIES

T.L. WAINWRIGHT

Taking a Chance
second edition. november 2021

Written by T.L Wainwright
This book was original published under the titles
breaking down the BARRICADE
The reed and rice series

Thank you.

T.L. Wainwright

CHAPTER 1

Amy

"Shh! Isaac," I groan quietly. "He's asleep." Motioning him out of our son's bedroom with a backward flip of my hands. I gently close the door behind us. Isaac stands as close as physically possible and slides his arms around my waist. Never a missed opportunity as his hands move up, cupping my breasts.

"God, I love your tits," he mumbles into my ear while giving them a quick squeeze. "Fuck, they're only going to get bigger now that you're pregnant again. Fucking A."

"Sometimes I think you only married me for my tits," I giggle, batting his hands away and trying to escape. He spins me around to face him and pulls me in even closer.

"Well, it was in the top five."

"Really, Mr Rice, and what were the other four?" I ask

as I gaze into his eye. I still find myself holding my breath as I fall into the chocolate depths.

"Well Mrs Rice, your ass," he grabs a handful of my butt and gives it a plumping. "Your lips." The softness of his mouth covers mine before sucking on my bottom lip, giving it a little nip with his teeth. He slides down onto his knees in front of me. "Your hot, sweet pussy," he pushes up the skirt of my dress. "That's always so wet and greedy for me." He nuzzles his face into the apex of my legs and inhales. "You smell so fucking good." I let out a whimper of disappointment as he jumps back up to his feet. "But most of all," he takes me into his embrace, a glint of sincerity on his face, "and number one on the list, is because you launder my shirts perfectly."

"You arsehole." I push at his chest with my clenched fist, but he holds onto me tighter.

"I love it when you get all prissy," he growls. "It makes my dick hard."

"Fuck you, Isaac."

"Shh! You'll wake Sam up." He runs his hands down my back, holds me just firm enough so I can't escape, and grins at me, like a naughty schoolboy. "I'm messing with you. I married you because my life could never and would never be the same without you. You've accepted me for who I am, my past and my present. We have a beautiful family and this little one," he rubs his hand across the slight roundness of my stomach. "Girl or boy, it too will be loved and protected with everything I have." His kiss is deep and meaningful. "Amy, you and the kids are my world." He turns me away from him and smacks me hard on the arse. "Now get your butt into that bedroom and I will prove to you how much I fucking love you."

"Have you spoken to Petra recently?" Isaac asks as he lays flat on his back, his arm wrapped around my shoulder, holding me close. My head rests on his chest and I can hear the comforting thump of his heartbeat.

"Now you mention it, not much," I lazily trace the indent of his abs with my index finger. "Not since she got back, anyway. Why do you ask?"

"Mmm, strange." He strokes my bare back with the flat of his hand. Goose bumps pop up across my skin, as little electric currents rush through my body. He still has this effect on me, lighting the touch paper and sending my body into a spin like a Catherine wheel on bonfire night. "Cade still has a stick up his ass over something, and his behaviour seems to get even worse. Did you ever find out what went on between them?"

"No, which is really weird."

"In what way?"

"Well, you know Kat, she's the one who keeps her private life private, but Petra. She's the reason TMI was invented."

"TMI?"

"Too much information. Come on Isaac," I tut. "Get with the programme. Something happened at our wedding. Hell, they were all over each other. I asked her, but she clammed up quicker than a Venus flytrap that had just caught lunch. Kat even tried to get her to spill the beans, and they've been friends for ages, but she ain't giving it up."

"I got a phone call from Ben the other day. He's worried about Cade. Apparently, he's either in the gym or out knocking back Bourbon in some seedy bar."

"Really?" I push myself up and face Isaac. His face tells me he's beginning to have his own concerns.

"Ben's concerned about the company he's keeping. Rumour has it, he's been fucking around too, a lot. Turning into a right man-whore." Isaac lets out a sigh as he grabs the hair on the top of his head.

"Hark at the pan calling the kettle grimy arse."

"What the hell are you saying, woman?" Isaac's expression now shows his confusion.

"You, calling Cade a man-whore." I pull his hand away from his head and smooth his hair back down with my own fingers. "Your reputation is hardly whiter than white, mister."

"I'm a hot-blooded man. Needs must," grabbing my hand and bringing it to his lips, he brushes a gentle kiss on the tips of my fingers. "But now I have you."

"So that's the real reason you married me. Sex on tap." I feign annoyance, rolling away from him and presenting him with my back.

"Don't think you can get away from me that easy," he pulls me roughly to him. "Didn't our vows say something about sex do us part?"

"Death, death and that will not be far off if you carry on, matey." I slap the arm that's wrapped securely around me. "What do you think you are doing?" I ask, as his leg pushes between mine. His hand circles my calf, lifting it so he can nestle in-between them. Bringing his knee up higher, he puts pressure on the apex of my legs. I am, for all intents and purposes, straddling his thigh. He rubs against me, my bare pussy firmly pressed against the hard muscle, and I'm instantly wet. As his hand kneads my breast, an overwhelming need for more friction against my clit has me rocking my body against him.

"You know exactly what I'm doing," Isaac whispers in my ear. "The way your body reacts to my touch. A single kiss from me still brings a flash of blush to your skin. When you look at me, all I see is your love for me etched across your face." He brushes his lips against the pulse point at my neck. "No one has ever looked at me the way you do. It makes my heart skip. It makes me feel like the fucking luckiest man in the world."

His hard cock presses against my lower back, so I reposition myself, telling him exactly what I want. As his hardness pushes in, he teases my clit, rolling the already excited nub between his skilful fingers. I take a deep breath, the sensation of him inside me still as exquisite as it was the very first time. The force of his thrusts starts off gentle and with precision, and I'm not sure if it's so I get to feel all of him, or if it's his need for all of me. Gradually, he speeds up until they become quick hard thrusts, but still with deep penetration.

"Isaac!" His name comes out a little garbled as I exhale it on a moan. I begin to tremble as I get closer and closer to the endgame.

"Amy," Isaac pants. "I'm so close. Come for me, baby."

His words are all it takes to push me over the edge. My inner muscles pulsate around his cock, gripping him hard. His body becomes rigid, and his jaw tightens, as deep animalistic sounds spill from his mouth and the warmth of his seed fills me as he finds his release.

Isaac rolls away from me, laying on his back, and I follow suit. Both of us try to catch our breath. A shimmer of moisture covers our bodies, and I'm instantly grateful for the cool air that flits across my hot skin.

"This will never falter," Isaac murmurs.

"The hot sexy?" He turns and looks at me, his hand sweeping away the stray hairs that are stuck to the moisture on my forehead.

"No. The irrefutable love that I have for you." He kisses me hard. A kiss that affirms his declaration. "I love you so much that… I feel it… right here," he pats the centre of his chest. "When I take in you and the kids, it's like my heart is about to burst with love, pride and admiration. You are my world; you know that, Amy?"

"I do, Isaac." I place the palm of my hand against his cheek, rubbing my thumb across the bone. "But what about the sex?" I turn to eye him, doing my best to keep my serious face. "Are you still going to shag me senseless when we're old?"

"Woman! I'm pouring my heart out here," he says, lifting his hand in exasperation before bringing it down with a gentle slap on my bum. "And all you are worried about is if I'll still find you attractive."

"Well actually, I was thinking more about if you'll still be able to get it up?"

"You cheeky bugger!" he shrieks with a really poor attempt at a Yorkshire accent. His fingers find my ticklish spot, the bit just under the ribs, but before you hit the hip bone, and he is relentless.

"No. NO!" I squeal, laughing loud and hard, twisting my body as I try to get away from his probing hands, but it's useless. "Isaaaaccccc! Please, you'll wake our boy."

With some reluctance, he lets me go, laughing, the smile on his face still laced with a hint of mischief. He hovers over me, a hand on each side of my head, as he leans in, stealing a heady kiss. "I'm going to take a quick shower." He walks away from the bed and I growl at the sight of his perfectly pert backside. He gives his bum a wiggle and winks at me over his shoulder before disappearing into the bathroom. Just after the shower water turns on, he bobs his head around the door. "Will you speak to Petra? See if you can find out what's going on?"

"Sure. I'll call her tomorrow. Are you going to call Cade?"

"He's flying over Friday to talk about a new acquisition we've been looking at."

"I thought he'd re-scheduled again?"

"He did, but I re-scheduled it right back. I'm not sure if it's me he's avoiding or something else."

"More like someone else," I correct.

"Either way, he's getting his ass here, whether he likes it or not. I'll talk to him then. Face to face is better because I can read him like a book. I'll be able to tell if he's hiding something."

He disappears back into the bathroom.

I wait until I hear the shower running before I follow him. The image of his body through the steamed-up glass is a little distorted, but no less spectacular. Opening the door, I slide in behind him and wrap my arms around his waist, pushing my boobs against the hard muscle of his back.

"Happy anniversary, Isaac." He turns to face me and pulls me further under the spray of the water. Our hair becomes plastered to our heads, as drops of water run down our faces. His kiss is filled with a thousand 'I love you's'. His tongue slipping between my lips, tells a million 'I want you's'. Our hearts beat together, declaring our 'forever yours'.

"Happy anniversary, beautiful," he whispers against my lips, and then the love making starts all over again.

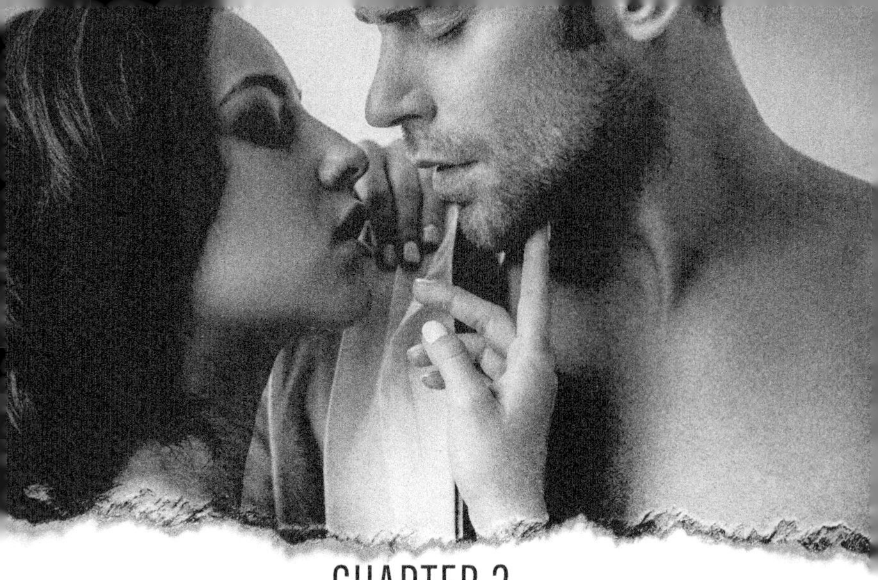

CHAPTER 2

Amy and Isaac's wedding
Two years earlier.

Petra

After a beautiful ceremony at Isaac's parents' house, the wedding party had moved to a grand hotel nearby. Isaac was insistent about it. For one, he had argued; he didn't want Jack and Kath to have all the stress when it came to the catering and stuff. And two, the house wasn't big enough to accommodate all the guests that would stay overnight. The decision to have the reception at the hotel was a clever move really, as now, most of us who plan to take advantage of the bar are in crawling distance from our beds. I guess it makes sense.

"Congratulations Amy, you are absolutely stunning."

The ivory dress that Amy is wearing frames her figure perfectly. It's long and fitted, but fans out from the hip down. Full soft folds of delicate silk pushed out by the layers of tulle underneath. It accentuates her boobs and waist in the best possible way, showing her sexy hourglass figure. The crystal beading on the bodice keeps catching the light, making her sparkle like a Disney princess.

"Ah thanks, Petra. I'll be honest, I do feel pretty in this gown," she does a little wiggle. "I'm not sure how the hell I'm going to hold all this fabric up when I go for a pee."

"I'm sure Isaac won't have any problems later, when he's desperate to get into your knickers," I giggle. "You look scrummy. It's taking me all my time to keep my hands off you." I give her a cheeky wink.

"You are so bad," Amy frowns, but then we hug it out before I move on.

"Petra," Isaac greets me with a gentle kiss on my cheek. "Thank you for coming. You, Kat, and Amy's other friends from home have made it so special for her. I'm really grateful."

"Congratulations, Isaac. I wouldn't have missed it for the world." I hold my hand out to him, he takes it even though he looks a little confused. I squeeze his hand hard. Well, hard for me anyway, and lean in a little closer so only he can hear. "You break her heart; I'll break your balls." He coughs out a nervous laugh, as I lean back and give him a perfect, forced smile. It's not that I don't like you Isaac, I do. But Amy's been through enough and us girls need to stick together.

"Petra, I don't doubt that for one minute, but believe

me when I say, I have no intention of hurting her, ever." I raise an eyebrow at him. "Never again," he corrects. "Never again. She's my everything." I give him a nod and a genuine smile.

"Hey Isaac, sounds like I need to be careful not to upset this friend of Amy's?"

I glance to Isaac's left to find the gorgeous specimen of a man that I've been eyeing up through most of the wedding ceremony. The fitty that I believe to be one of Isaacs's brothers. Amy has spoken of him before, but up until today, I had never met him.

"Ah yes, of course, you two haven't been introduced yet." Isaac turns to his brother. "This little firecracker is Petra, now don't be deceived by that angelic face of hers. She's one hell of a spunky lady."

"God, I so hate that word 'spunky'," I chip in.

"Okay, feisty is that better?" Isaac offers.

"I'll take that," I grin.

"This is my brother, Cade. I'm trying to convince him to come work for me, to head up a Legal team, but he's having none of it. You could put in a good word for me?"

I give Cade a slow, exaggerated head to toe once over before I comment.

"Looks to me like he's big enough to make his own decisions." I smile sweetly and hold out my hand. "Hi Cade,"

"Feisty?" he takes my hand, his fingers curling around it, his hold firm but gentle. "Hi Petra, it's lovely to meet you."

Not being of any great stature, and Cade at least a good

foot taller, I have to tilt my head to meet his incredibly blue eyes. I can tell that he's smiling, because of the tiny creases at the corner of his eyes, but I can't, for the life of me, redirect my gaze. Fuck me! If his eyes were lagoons, I'd be stripped naked and splashing about in them in a nanosecond.

"So, Petra, you work for Isaac?" Cade asks, as I take in the rest of his beautiful face. He's got those classic American, handsome, strong chiselled features. Almost a cowboy-esque air about him, which has me wondering… is he more Unforgiven or Brokeback Mountain?

"Cade, you're holding up the line here," Isaac growls quietly from the corner of his mouth. I see Kat is next in line. She's gorgeous, with her cat like features, tall, slim and legs long enough to wrap around the hunk of magnificent meat that stood right in front of me. Suddenly, I feel small and insignificant. It's not Kat's fault that she's naturally flawless.

"Damn!" Cade cusses under his breath. "Duty calls." It's when he pulls me slightly nearer to him I realise he still has hold of my hand. "I'll catch-up with you later. I'd really like to find out if what my brother says is accurate." A offers a wink and he slowly releases my hand and turns to the next in line. I stand there watching him, when I should be moving along until…

"Hi, I'm Ben." My head snaps around so fast that it's a wonder I don't get whiplash.

"Oh, yes. Hi Ben," I stutter. "You must be Isaac's other brother?"

"Mmm," he laughs. "Why am I constantly referred to as 'The other brother.'" he air marks.

"No! Did I hit a sore spot there?" I titter. "I'm sorry… Ben, The Brother, I'm Petra, a friend of Amy's and I have the delight of having your 'other brother' as my boss."

"Don't tell me you don't like Isaac?"

"Actually, Isaac is one of the good ones. I've had worse."

"Mmm, he can still be a bit of an arsehole."

"I think it's a requirement for Boss status."

"You're very…"

"Ben!" Cade growls. "People are waiting."

"Chill, man," Ben replies, but keeping his attention on me. "We can have a drink, chat a little more, once all this meet and greet stuff is done with?"

"BEN!" Cade's face is turning a dark shade of pissed off. "Move it."

"I'll catch up with you later," Ben sniggers, totally taking his time and making the most of getting on his brother's tits. He kisses my cheek and whispers, "I wouldn't mind chatting to your tall blonde friend as well."

"Of course," I shake my head, but not the least bit surprised.

After the wedding breakfast, both Kat and I stand in the bar area with a glass of champagne in one hand and balancing a napkin with two or three delicate works of art on the other.

"These desserts look like they have been constructed with micro precision." I watch Kat as she tries to work out how to get the food to her mouth without a free hand to grab it. I must admit, it's a little different to forgo the usual mountains of puddings and instead serve them a-la-canapé style. Fortunately, when Kat looks like she's going to go down on the sweet treats like she's bobbing for apples, Ben comes to the rescue.

"Let me take that for you," he says, taking the glass flute from her hand.

"Thank you," she replies before slipping a fancy lemon mini pastry into her mouth. "Oh. My. God. That's sooooo good."

"If you hadn't guessed, Ben, Kat has an affinity with food."

"I do not," Kat muffles behind her hand, strategically placed so we don't see the half-mushed mini-pud number two.

"Although you wouldn't believe it, skinny bitch." I elbow her on her side and she scowls at me when she nearly drops mini-pud number three. "Ben, would you mind entertaining Kat for a while? I need to nip to the loo." I pause for a moment before I walk away. "Oh, and please make sure she doesn't eat her body weight in mint macarons and peanut butter chocolate balls. We have drinking to do." Kat gives me one of her death stares, but doesn't say a word. Her mouth is full again, thanks to me placing my own laden napkin on top of her empty one. Kat never likes to see food wasted.

I wander off to find the toilets, when I spot a sign at the far side of the room, I make a beeline for it. I'm about to make it to the corridor when my pathway is blocked by Cade.

"Petra."

"I need to pee." I put my hand against his chest to push him out of my way. My 5'5" stature is no contest against his 5'11" solid lump of man muscle. But I'm bursting, and if I don't get to my destination fast, there's going to be one hell of an embarrassing situation. Possibly a clean-up on… mmm, carpet, reception area. "Desperately." I say firmly.

"Affirmative." Cade steps back, clearing my way. "Don't let me keep you from your mission."

I give him a 'Really' expression, shake my head and almost jog on down the corridor. It's not until I've safely sat my arse on the toilet seat and relieved some of the pressure that I allow myself to laugh out loud.

Cade

Affirmative. Keep you from your mission. What the fuck!

The hottest woman in the room has me talking like a dorky college kid, while my dick decides that he wants to be firmly between her glossy lips, nicely nestled in her hot, wet mouth. Fuck! She's sexy and that accent. Holy shit!

Don't get me wrong, I've had a few girls and even had a sort of relationship, if you can call seeing the same girl for six months a relationship. It was convenient at the time, I had my finals. Okay, I was using her a little. Yes, I was a bit of a jackass.

College life was a blast. I made the most of the time away from the family home with no restraints, beer and liquor flowing freely, and the constant supply of eager girls only too happy to ride my dick. Some of them had been smoking hot. Perky tits, tight ass and willing to try anything. Well, most things. Actually, nothing out of the ballpark. But the sex was good and, more importantly, regular.

Not one of them had ever grasped my attention the way this dark-haired, brown eyed, olive-skinned beauty has. The way the burnt orange, all in one, I think they call it a cat-suit, cuts low at the front. Not too much, that would be inappropriate for a wedding, not that it would bother me, but it shows the soft mounds of her pushed up boobs perfectly. God, I bet they look spectacular when released from their confinements. And that ass. God damn, the fabric creases nicely in between her cheeks, exactly where I'd like to rub my dick. Shit!

I should stay away from this girl. She works for my brother. She's a friend of Amy's. It has disaster written all over it.

So, why am I hanging around in the corridor, not more than a couple of metres from the ladies' restroom?

Petra

I'm head down, busy fiddling with the clasp on my bag when I stumble into Cade, literately. Grabbing my elbow, he steadies me as I waver, the heels I'm wearing being ridiculously high. They're not my usual choice of footwear when it's going to be a long day thing, but the legs of this pantsuit are too long for a more suitable heel, and I can't sew for the life of me.

"Woah, Cowboy!" I exhale, once I regain my balance. "Do you often hang around outside ladies' toilets waiting for women?"

"I don't tend to make a habit of it."

"You shouldn't," I chastise. "It's a little creepy." I can't help but be a little smug and flattered, however much it seems a little stalkerish. I move to go past him, but he still has hold of my arm, so he pulls me a little closer to him.

"I didn't want you to be monopolised by my brother, before I have the opportunity to get to find out more about you."

"I think Isaac is pretty tied up with his new bride. Hell, he's hardly taken his hands off her since she got to the altar."

"I was talking about Ben," he smiles, and it lights up his face. Hell, he's gorgeous. "How do you feel about having a drink with me while I do some subtle questioning?"

"Questioning or interrogation?" I snigger.

"I'm a lawyer, not the FBI," he steps to my side and puts his hand to the centre of my back, and I allow him to slowly lead me forward and back out amongst the other guests.

"Looks like your worries about Ben are unfounded." I point towards a table in the corner where Kat and Ben are happily chatting away. Kat gives nothing away to the untrained eye, but I know better. She likes him. However, if Ben can read her body language, maybe he should work for the FBI.

"Ben likes her, I can tell. I'm not so sure about your friend." He turns his attentions back to me. "What can I get you to drink?"

"I doubt if they'll have Tatratea, so I'll have a Vodka with ice. In regard to Kat, well, I've known her for years and she keeps her emotions well hidden."

"Hold that thought," he instructs, raising a finger in gesture. He turns and chats to the barman and I take the opportunity to check the room, looking for any other familiar faces. Very few of the guests are from work. I recognise Josh, who had been based out in Pittsburgh for a while, but has moved back to Bath with his lovely wife, who is currently pregnant with their second child. Layla, Josh and Cami's daughter, and flower girl for the day, stands beside them looking every bit the angel that she seems to be.

"There you go," Cade interrupts, handing me a tall glass with lots of ice and a substantial measure of amber liquid.

I take a sip a matter of seconds before Cade does.

"Mmm, Bohemian," I lick my lips as the hint of blueberries hits my taste buds.

Cade coughs and splutters, so I give him a couple of sharp slaps between his shoulder blades.

"Holy shit!" he chokes out. "What the fuck?" He holds the glass up and inspects the liquid before smelling it. "How, on God's earth do you drink this stuff?"

"Bohemian is 62% proof, so you ordered the potent stuff," I can't help but laugh as I take in his red face. I wave towards the bartender. "Is there any champagne left?" The bar tender nods and brings over two flutes. I pour some of the contents from one of them into Cade's glass. I grab a swizzle stick from a container on the bar and give it a quick stir. "Try it now."

Cade takes a tentative sip, then nods his head.

"Better?" I giggle, unable to hide my amusement.

"Much better," he laughs. "Shit, I think I just lost my drinking credibility."

"You should try Outlaw. That would really make you lose your shit," I tease. "They do make more subtle versions of Tatratea. Why don't you try coconut and work your way up?"

"That's a hard pass," he gripes out, grimacing at the glass in his hand. "I think I'll leave this devil's fire water where it should stay. In the bottle."

"This is one of my homeland's greatest creations and you're slagging it off?" I gasp with fake disapproval.

"Sorry," he grimaces, which makes me feel a little guilty for the teasing. "So, Amy tells me you're Slovakian?"

"You couldn't tell by my accent?"

"Would you be mad if I said that all Eastern European accents sound the same to me?" he says with a cringe, as if expecting an onslaught. I'm tempted, but I decide to cut back on the wind-up.

"I am a little, but seeing as I can't tell the difference between an American and a Canadian accent, I'll let you off."

"Touché!" Cade hits me with one of his amazing grins. I glance the other way before I go into meltdown. The urge to squeeze my thighs together is almost unquenchable. "Can I redeem myself a little, by telling you I find your English exceptional and your accent very sexy?"

"Maybe," I wonder why the room has suddenly become a lot warmer, then I realise I'm blushing. What is Cade doing to me? I don't do blushing. I need to take back control, so

I tilt my head to one side, drop my gaze to the floor slowly, then snap it right back up to meet his. This guy is getting my flirtatious side to the max. "I've been in the U.K. for years now. I've even picked up a few typical English phrases."

"I must admit, I struggle with some of them. Even Isaac still has to get Amy to interpret occasionally."

I take another sip of my drink, looking over the glass, making sure I keep eye contact. His gaze drops slightly, and he watches as I run the tip of my tongue across my lips, boosting the already glossy shine of my lipstick.

He steps a little closer.

"Have you come over to Florida just for the wedding?" His hand comes forward, fingers slipping under the fabric strap at my shoulder. I shiver at his touch. "Or are you staying a little longer?"

He teases the fabric between his fingers. His knuckles skim my skin, sending tingling sensations across my body. I swallow hard before I speak. "It seemed a shame not to get the most out of the nine-hour flight, so Kat and I decided to stay for the week." His hand moves further down, and his fingers brush the side of my breast. Forget tingles. Now I have a full-on power surge going straight to my suska. In other word's… vagina.

We stare at each other for a few moments. Everything around us seems fuzzy and insignificant. I go to take another drink, only to find that the glass is empty.

"I think I need another drink."

"Do you want the same again?"

"Why don't we stick with the champagne, if that's okay with you?"

"Excuse me, Sir," he shouts to the barman, but his eyes stay firmly fixed on me. "Two bottles of champagne please, but only uncork the one and four glasses." He picks up on my confused expression instantly. "Why don't we go join Kat and Ben? I'm sure they'll be happy to help us take care of these." He waves the two bottles in his hands. I thread my fingers through the stems of the glasses, three in one hand and the fourth in the other.

"What's up, Cowboy, getting bored with me already?" I question, raising an eyebrow.

"On the contrary," he leans in and whispers. "I'm trying to be a gentleman, and the best way to keep me in check is for you to have a couple of chaperones."

Cade

I make sure I'm behind Petra when we walk over to the table where my brother, Ben is sitting with Kat. That way, I get the perfect view of her round ass. If I didn't have my hands full, I'd be tempted to touch. Kat and Ben must be getting along, because their heads are quite close together and they're laughing.

"Hi, you two, are you going to let us in on the joke?" I hear Petra ask.

"I'm not sure that we should?" Ben replies, tapping his bottom lip with his index finger. "What do you think, Kat?"

"We have champagne." I hold out the two bottles.

"I have glasses," Petra adds to my attempt at bribery.

"In that case, you absolutely get my vote," Kat giggles.

"I guess you better take a seat," Ben stands, and pulls out a chair for Petra as she places the glasses on the table. "And you brother, better pour."

Ben explains he was recounting some of our childhood antics. Most of which I ended up being the butt of the joke. By the time we had finished the second bottle and had gained a third from the bar, Ben had got to our teenage years.

When he started the story about my first sexual experience, I shoot him a stare that clearly says, shut the fuck up or I'm going to rip you a new asshole. The problem is, Ben never knows when to stop. His mouth goes faster than his brain and the fact that he's pissed doesn't help the situation. So, he just carries on.

"Oh, no!" Petra is laughing so hard that she can hardly get the words out. "Your first time going down on a girl..." she struggles to get her breath, "and she farted?"

I rub my hand down my face, exasperated. This is not how I envisioned this going.

"And you ran?" Petra is now holding her stomach, her laughter uncontrollable and gaining us more and more attention. "That is so fucking hilarious."

"Shh! Come on, give me a break." I try to explain myself. "I was only sixteen and was as nervous as shit."

"Scared by a queef," Petra's not letting it go. She's pretty well gone herself, and her words are a little slurred. "You do know that if queefs were skittles, you might have tasted the rainbow."

"What the fuck?" I can't help but laugh along with her crazy comment. "You, lady, are trouble."

"You, Cowboy, are an Ancraommm, an Ancraofff,"

stopping, unable to say the word she's so desperately trying to say, she takes a glug of champagne, a deep breath and then slurs out, "an Ancraophobic!"

"And what's that?" Ben asks.

"Scared of wind," Kat sniggers.

Petra laughs and snorts at the same time as taking another drink. Not a good move. She suddenly starts coughing and spluttering, but still continues to giggle.

"I need a pee," she stands, now having regained some composure.

"I'll come with you," Kat announces, standing and linking her arm in with Petra's before they walk in the general direction of the bathrooms.

"Back in a sec," Petra shouts over her shoulder, almost toppling over in the process. Kat steadies her, much less affected by the alcohol we've consumed.

"Kat's awesome," Ben announces as soon as they are out of earshot. "She sure can eat. And look at her, you'd never had guessed that she's drunk over a bottle of champagne."

"Can't say the same for Petra," I laugh.

"She seems pretty cool to me," Ben scowls.

"No, I didn't mean that. I didn't see her eat much at dinner, yet she's been knocking back the drink. She's cool. And pissed."

"You were watching her?" Ben sniggers. "Jesus, you really like her, don't you?"

"She's… nice."

"Cade. Don't be an ass. You really like her, I can tell."
I'm about to defend myself when I see them out of the corner of my eye. Well, not really. I've been watching, waiting for

her to return like a pining puppy.

"Shut the fuck up, they're coming back," I hiss between clenched teeth.

"I think this one has had enough," Kat announces as she struggles to keep Petra upright. "I'm going to take her up to her room." Both Ben and I stand. I put my arm firmly around Petra to take some of the strain from Kat. Well, kinda.

"You're both staying here?" I ask.

"Yes. Isaac's thought of everything. He's far too generous for his own good."

"Are you and Petra sharing a room?" Strange question, but I have my reasons.

"Are you kidding me?" Kat smirks. "We were more than willing to share, but no, Isaac booked us our own rooms. Looks like that's going to be a waste of money." I frown at her, a little confused. "I can't leave her on her own like this. She's wasted," she explains further.

"Why don't we take her to her room. You can get her…" I wave my hands up and down, gesturing at Petra's body, "undressed." I swallow hard at the thought of being the one to strip her. But I'm determined to be a gentleman. "Once she's settled in bed, I'll be happy to sit with her."

"I, mmm, I'm not sure." Kat looks dubious but also a little tempted.

"Stay, Kat," Ben interjected. "Cade will keep an eye on her. I was hoping to at least get one dance with you before the end of the night." When Ben gives her the puppy eyes and pushes out his bottom lip, she concedes.

"Okay," she sighs. "Help me get her upstairs," she points at me with her free hand. "And you," she nods at

Ben. "Get the drinks in. I'll be back in a few minutes."

"Yes ma'am," we both reply at the same time

CHAPTER 3

Cade

Once we've left Ben at the bar, we take the elevator up to the fourth floor. When the doors slide open, I quickly check that the hallway is clear before I scoop Petra up into my arms. She's pretty much out of it, but her arms wrap around my neck, her head falling against my shoulder.

"Yuw shmell nicesh," she slurs, snuggling into my neck. "Ako chlap (like a man)."

"Thank you," I reply. "I think." I glance over at Kat, and she's sniggering.

Kat gets the key card out of Petra's purse and swipes it. The red light turns to green, so she pushes open the door, stands back, and allows me enough space to walk into the room.

They have left one of the bedside lamps on, so the subtle

light is enough for me to make out the layout of the room.

It's nice. A good size with everything you would expect from a five-star establishment. However, I don't waste my time mulling over the décor, I head straight to the bed.

I lay Petra down and step back away from the bed.

"Right," Kat looks at me. I just stand there. "At least turn your back or step out of the room or something while I undress her."

"Oh, yes," I nervously scan the room. "The bathroom." I point to the door.

"Well, go on," she waves at me when I still don't move from the spot. "I'll shout when it's safe to come out."

"Yeah, yeah," I nod as move away into the bathroom, closing the door behind me.

I glance at my reflection in the mirror, and it's a little distorted. I've consumed more alcohol than I usually do. I'm more of a beer and bourbon man, and the champagne has definitely had an effect on me.

I can hear a muffled voice from the other side of the door, and I turn to face it. My mind begins to work overtime, visualising what I might see if it wasn't for that damn door. Fuck! I bet Petra's as hot as hell in a bra and panties. My cock thinks so too and starts getting past the semi-hard state that has been present since I first set eyes on her. "Shit!" I breathe as I palm my pants, partly to ease some of the pressure, but also to push my dick into a position where my predicament is less obvious.

The bathroom door opens and Kat raises her eyebrows, catching me with my hands at the front of my pants.

"You can come out now," she says. "That's if you're

not otherwise engaged?" I'm sure I hear her snigger, before she turns her back to me and returns to the side of the bed. "She's out of it."

"Hopefully she'll sleep it off," I add.

"Hopefully," Kat concurs. "But keep an eye on her for a couple of hours. Just in case."

"Just in case?"

"If she wakes up suddenly, make sure you get her to the bathroom, real quick."

"Oh!" I grimace.

"Yep, because you'll be in charge of clean-up if you don't."

"Shit!"

"Look, if you don't think you can handle it, I'll stay with her." Kat says the words, but I can tell that she's itching to get back downstairs. To Ben.

"I'll be fine," I assure her. Well, I wouldn't be much of a brother if I let my little bro miss out. It's blatantly obvious that Ben has the hots for Kat.

"Are you sure?" she asks with a tentative smile. I reply with a definitive nod. "Okay, give me your phone." I hand it to her but she hands me it straight back. "Unlock please." I do as she says, then she holds it in her hands, both thumbs punching at the screen. "There," she hands it back. "I'm sure everything will be fine, but if you have any problems, ring me and I'll come straight up. If it's late, then I'm right down the hall, room 412."

"Thanks." I smile back at her, her assurance making me feel less apprehensive. "I'll take care of her, don't worry."

"Okay then. I'm off to find Ben. Fingers crossed," She

holds her hand up and yes, she has her fingers crossed. "I won't see you until the morning."

I follow Kat to the door, holding it open and linger in the doorway until I see her disappear into the elevator. Securing the door, I move over to the window and haul the chair that's there closer to the bed, before I hang my jacket on the back. Once I've removed my wristwatch and cufflinks, I place them on the bedside cabinet before rolling up my shirt sleeves, ready to sit and watch.

She's laid on her side facing me, all curled up with her eyes shut tight. Her hands that are together, palm against palm, as if in prayer, are tucked under her flushed cheek. Lips slightly upturned in the softest of smiles, making me wonder what it is she might be thankful for. Her dark, luxurious hair fans across the crisp white cotton pillow. The contrast between dark and light is immense. She shuffles under the light sheet that covers her body, causing the fabric to slide slowly down her shoulder, giving me a teasing peek at the curve of her slender neck. Her mouth moves and a soft mumbling escapes her lips. It's so sudden that I can't quite work out the words. As quick as it came, it's gone, and she falls back into her drunken dream.

My chin hits my chest, causing me to suddenly become alert and I realise I was falling asleep. I pull my phone out of my pocket and scroll through the screens until I get to the Walking Dead game app. As soon as I click it, the noise of the intro music has me mentally kicking myself as I quickly try to turn down the volume. "Shit, shit, shit!"

"What are you doing here, Cowboy?" Petra's voice immediately gets my attention and I find her laid on her back, eyes shut, her arms above her head as she stretches. My cock instantly becomes active when I see the sheet has fallen to her waist, giving me the perfect view of her olive skin against the ivory bra. Exquisite.

"I drew the short straw," I laugh softly. "I got babysitting duty."

"Lucky you. Kat's doing no doubt."

"It's a cross I'm willing to bare."

Her arms come back down, and she rolls to face me. She can barely open her eyes. "Come closer, I can hardly see you." She says, patting the space on the edge of the bed.

I hesitate for a moment, then get up and sit beside her.

"You smell nice," she murmurs. "All sexy and manly."

"I don't know what to say to that," I say, brushing my hand through my hair. "Thank you?"

"You're welcome," she places her hand on my thigh. Instantly, the heat permeates the fabric of my dress pants. "You look good in a suit, but I'd love to see you in less." The touch of her fingers as they skim up and down my leg does nothing to help with the hardening cock situation.

"I think you should try to get some sleep," I reply sterner than I intend. I put my hand over hers. God, the temptation to move it further up, is excruciating. But I don't. I place it back at the side of her.

"I'm sure I would if you got in with me."

"That's not going to happen."

"Why not?" she looks at me again with one eye open, then closes it again. A kind of wink.

"Because you've had a lot to drink, and I'm not sure I could control myself. I will not take advantage of this situation."

"You've had a lot to drink too, so it makes us even. Besides, maybe it's me that wants to take advantage of you." I smile and shake my head, but it gets quickly wiped off my face when she pulls back the cotton sheet. An open invitation. "Come on, get in with me."

"Like I said," A hint of vanilla wafts towards me, invading my senses when I lean over, grab the sheet and pull it back over her. The bad voice in my head curses me out for being such a pussy. The good voice doesn't seem to intervene, but I stay determined. "It's not going to happen, so you may as well go to sleep."

"If you don't get in, then I'm going to keep on talking and talking until you're sick of hearing me. Then you'll have no choice but to do as I say."

"Has anyone ever told you that you're bossy when you're drunk? Anyway, that's not going to work either," I chuckle. "Have you forgotten that I like the sound of your voice?"

"Oh, shit. You're no fun, are you?" Petra falls on to her back, exasperated.

"On the contrary, I can be lots of fun."

"Is there nothing I can do to tempt you?" she asks in a slight slurred, but still sexy, sultry voice.

"Believe me, I'm tempted and if circumstances were different, I wouldn't need to be asked once, never mind twice."

"Steady on, Cowboy. You can't tease a girl like that and then give her nothing," she sighs. "What about a kiss?"

"Petra."

"One kiss and I promise, I'll go straight to sleep." With her eyes still closed, she angles her head towards me and puckers her soft pink lips.

The temptation is too much and I lean in and touch her mouth with mine. I was going to make it a quick kiss, but the softness of her lips has me staying for longer than I intended. A soft moan vibrates in her throat and I increase the force of the kiss, teasing her mouth open with my tongue.

Petra suddenly breaks away, hurriedly sitting up and causing our heads to clash.

"Ouch!" she groans, rubbing at the bumped spot. "I think I'm going to be sick."

"Grab hold," I almost shout as I pull back the sheet and scoop her up. I move as fast as I can, trying to ignore the fact that I have a half-naked woman in my arms. Kicking the bathroom door open with my foot, I step up to the toilet before I let her feet touch the ground. I hear the unmistakable sound of hurling, followed by a warm, wet sensation on my chest, as she vomits down the front of my shirt.

Her eyes are huge and apologetic as she looks up at me before she spins around and drops onto her knees in front of the toilet. Quickly, I grab handfuls of her hair, and pull it back, holding it in place as she continues to hurl. Gently, I rub her shoulders, patiently waiting for the sickness to subside.

I notice a hair tie on the vanity. I pick it up and secure her hair in place. Unbuttoning my dress shirt, I pull it from me carefully, roll it up and toss it into the bathtub. When I find a couple of washcloths, I wet them both. One, I add soap to and quickly wipe myself down. The other, I keep close at hand.

"I'm sorry," Petra says quietly as she turns and sits cross-legged on the cold tiled floor. "How to lose a guy in one day, eh!"

"Ah! But I'm still here." I lower myself down, push the strands of hair from her face and slowly wipe the damp cloth across her forehead. "How are you feeling?"

"Stupid," she huffs. "But better."

"Wait here a second." I walk back into the main room and grab a bottle of water from the minibar.

"I wasn't thinking of going anywhere," I hear her comment.

"Good, because you need to hydrate." I remove the lid and pass her the bottle. "Small sips. Let's test the waters first. Make sure that you don't bring it straight back up."

"Ha! Test the waters… funny."

"I'm not trying to be funny. I'm trying to make you better."

She takes a few small sips and hands me the bottle back. She shivers.

"Shit, you must be freezing on that floor." I hold out my hand to her and she takes it. Gently I pull her to her feet, but she wavers a little, so I scoop her up again. Her chilled skin feels good under my fingers. This time, I take her slowly back to the bed.

When I lower her down onto the edge of the bed, her arms stay firmly around my neck.

"Stay with me," she murmurs. "You don't need to get under the covers, just be here."

"Okay," I bring her arms away from my neck. "Shove

up." Once she's at the far side of the bed, I grab the sheet and pull it over her, tucking it close to her body. With both hands I plump up the spare pillow and place it against the headboard before resting against it with my legs flat out in front of me.

Petra's body shakes.

"Are you still cold?"

"Freeeezzzing!" she says between chattering teeth.

I hold up my arm and motion for her to come closer. Immediately, she shifts across the bed and snuggles into my side. The touch of her hand as she lays it against my bare chest is electric and I fail to stop myself from pulling her in even closer still. I try to tell myself that it's simply to share my body heat to warm her. The genuine reason is because holding her is so fucking good.

The soft murmurs of approval as she shakes, begin to subside along with the touch of her nearly naked body pressed up close to mine, has my head spinning and my dick pushing hard against the zipper of my pants. I consider taking the pillow from behind my head to place it over my lap, but I think that it would highlight the predicament that I'm in.

I glance down at her face that's now resting on my chest. Her eyes are closed and her mouth is slightly open, her breathing soft and regular. Thank God, she's drifted off to sleep.

CHAPTER 4

Petra

My first thought when I wake up, laid flat on my stomach with my face planted in the pillow, is… 'Fuck! My head.' It feels like someone has used it as a punch ball and the stuffing is about to explode out of it.

My second; nice. When I turn my head to find Cade asleep at the side of me, shirtless, but at least he's still got his trousers on. Actually, I'm not 100% sure if that's a positive or a negative. Well, hell, he is gorgeous. And fit. And very well put together, if my memory hasn't failed me.

My third? Holy shit! If my memory serves me right, I was a total mess last night.

"For fuck's sake!" I whisper to myself. "For once, couldn't it have just been a bloody dream?"

"Is this a regular thing for you?" Cade's voice makes

me jump.

"Making a total arse of myself when I drink? A little too often." I sit up, pulling the sheet up to my chin as soon as I register the state of my undress. "Waking up with strange men in my bed? Not so much."

"That's good to know." He slides off the bed, stands and stretches. "And for the record, you didn't make a total ass of yourself, maybe a little."

"Come on," I huff. "I threw up on you. How arseholery is that?"

"So, you remember most of what happened last night?"

"Not everything." I side glance at him, my skin becoming warm with embarrassment. "Did you take my clothes off?"

"Regrettably, I did not," he sighs, before turning towards the bathroom. "Kat did." He shouts over his shoulder before disappearing through the door.

I quickly jump out of bed, only to be stopped in my tracks by the pounding in my head. Moving slower than I'd like to, I grab a baggy t-shirt from my suitcase that's sitting on one of those folding thingy's that you always find in hotels, and pull it over my head. It barely covers my bum, but at least it's a little less revealing.

"By any chance, do you have a spare one of those for me?" Cade asks. He's stood in the bathroom doorway, his blonde hair a little ruffled, his trousers creased and a scruff of hair on his chin. Even the slight hint of shadows under his eyes from his lack of sleep takes nothing away from his good looks. Hell, I'd do him. That's if I ever got the chance again. Who am I kidding, I'd never have the balls to.

Champagne should have a warning label on the side. 'Too much can seriously turn you into a drunken lush. Especially if you're called Petra.'

"I do, but I'm not sure if it will fit you." I pull out a pink top which I use for sleeping in, which has bold black lettering saying, 'Does this shirt make my tits look big?' in a sort of 3D effect, so it actually does make your boobs seem two sizes bigger.

"Why would you buy that?" he laughs. "You're hardly… small."

"Kat got me it. Bit of a joke between us, with her only having diddy ones." I laugh back, then have to hold my head to stop the banging. "I got her back. Gave her one that had two large hands over the boobs and the words 'No Silicone'."

"You must be great friends?"

"The best," I reply, throwing the shirt towards him.

He holds it up to take another look before rolling it and tosses it back.

"Thanks, but pink's not my colour. I think I'll just fasten my jacket up until I get back to my room."

"What floor are you on?" I hear my inner nosey ask.

"14th,"

"That's high up," I gasp. "Wait, that's the top floor. You've got one of the posh suites? They're meant to be lush."

"It's okay, I guess," he smiles. "Why don't I wait here for you to get ready for breakfast, then you can come and check it out while I get changed."

"Really?" I give out an embarrassing squeal. "Give me

ten minutes,"

"Yeah," he raises an eyebrow, clearly not believing that I can get ready so quick. But he underestimates me. I'm unstoppable, especially when I get to indulge my unusual secret obsession.

I walk over to him, forcefully pushing him towards the bed and make him sit. "Wait here. Don't move. Ten minutes." Then I grab clean underwear, jeans and a light jumper from my suitcase and disappear into the bathroom.

I double brush my teeth while in the shower, making sure I get rid of the icky taste from my mouth. I dry off, get dressed and scrape my damp hair into a high ponytail in record time. A quick coat of tinted moisturiser, flick of the blusher brush and a layer of mascara, helps to make me look half human. Mint balm gives my lips a soft gloss, the finishing touch. I swallow down a couple of painkillers, then step back out of the bathroom.

"Wow!" is my greeting, when Cade looks up from his phone. I'm a little surprised that he's actually still sat in the same spot. "Most women would take hours and still wouldn't look half as good as you."

"Why thank you sir," I give a little cute curtsy to distract from my ridiculous blushing. Yes, blushing again, what the? "I need to grab some shoes." Normally I'd grab a pair of flats, but my hands seem to have a mind of their own when they pick up a pair of high wedges and start slipping them onto my feet.

"Ready?" Cade asks from right behind me.

"Shit! Cowboy, do you creep up on people all the time?"

"No, just you. It's kinda funny when you do that little

jump thing." He walks over and opens the door, standing back and waiting for me to go first.

We don't really speak much on the ride up in the lift. It's a little awkward, but not massively uncomfortable. I watch him out of the corner of my eye and when I think he's not looking; I try to sneak a better look. He sure can wear a suit and the fact that he's minus a shirt, I'm half expecting him to start gyrating, slowly sliding off his jacket, before ripping off his trousers in one super-fast movement, like he's one of the Dream Boys. I wonder if his trousers have Velcro seams. The fantasy in my head has me distracted and I miss the fact that he's now watching me, watching him. He has a big arse, smug as shit, smile on his face because he's caught me.

"What?" I snap, annoyed at getting caught. Then the lift stops and the door opens. He doesn't reply, just smiles some more and gestures for me to step out first.

I follow him until he stops outside a door a little way down the hall. Swiping his card, again being the perfect gentleman, he pushes open the door, then stands back waiting for me to enter.

When he flicks on the light, I become consumed by the vision.

Beautiful dark hard wood flooring. A window that covers most of one wall. Plush fabrics, fine furniture and expensive looking accessories. Most of the room is in earthy colours, but then given a vibrant splash of citrus green with the use of lamps, rugs and wall canvases. Hotel opulence like I've never seen before.

I step further into the living area of the suite, running

my fingers along the hard-looking leather of the sofa, which is as soft as butter to the touch.

I spy double doors off to one side of the room. I glance back at Cade, a silent ask for permission.

"Go ahead," he replies.

I almost skip towards them but stop for a moment, caressing the crystal knobs on the door. I take a deep breath in anticipation of what I'm about to see before I twist and push the doors wide open.

"Holy shit!" I gasp, taking in the beauty. Like most hotel bedrooms, it's dominated by the enormous bed. The colour scheme of the luxurious bedding mirrors the one in the living room, but with the addition of the crisp white sheets and pillows. A large dresser sits against the wall, that's adjacent to another floor to ceiling window, which is draped with a soft, light defusing organza curtain. I walk around the bed, letting my fingers trail across the fabrics, touching the wood at the head, before I check out the texture of the shade that sits proudly on the bedside lamp.

"Am I missing something here?" Cade asks, snapping me out of my interior love fest.

"Oh, err, I'm just looking."

"It's more than that," he laughs softly, "the expression on your face, it's like..."

"Like what?" I turn to face him.

"Nothing, nothing, ignore me." He waves it away, turns his back to me and moves toward the window, looking out. The silence is palpable, and I wonder if he's more sensitive guy than hard man.

"Okay, if you must know," I break the silence with a

huff. “I have this thing about hotel rooms.” He looks over his shoulder at me and winks.

“Now this could be interesting.”

“Not in that way, you dog.” I blush a little. What is it with this blushing malarkey? “The design, the way they put together the room with colours, fabrics and the furniture.” I walk over and stand beside him. “For example,” I point into the room. “See how they’ve taken the earth colours, the wood, the bright white, then a hint of lime? It reminds me of a walk in the country in summer. Then you turn and glance out of the window and you see the light sand, the ocean, the motion of the waves and you’re now holidaying at the beach.” I let out a contented sigh. “Different aspects, yet so absolutely perfect.”

It’s my turn to catch him watching me, and the way he’s looking at me has my skin tingling. Neither of us seems able to take our eyes off the other.

“Did I say something wrong?” My voice is so quiet, I scarcely hear it myself.

“Not at all,” he replies. “You surprised me a little.”

“That I turned out to be some weirdo hotel stalker,” I laugh. “I rarely get to see rooms that are as opulent as this. I find it interesting, that’s all.”

“I see a reasonably pleasant hotel room. You see, the detail.” He walks over to the dresser, removes his wallet and phone from his pocket and lays them on the surface. “I’m starving, but I need to grab a quick shower. You don’t mind, do you? I’ll stick to the ten-minute target you set.”

“No problem, but can I check out the bathroom first?”

Code

I leave her to check out the bathroom, while I remove my jacket, shoes, and socks, leaving me in just my dress pants.

"Wow!" Petra exhales, appearing in the doorway. I'm as proud as a peacock at her reaction to seeing me again in a state of undress, I take a step towards her when she says, "The floor and wall tiles are exactly what I would have put with this suite, and the shower is something else." She's so excited that I'm surprised she's stopped to take a breath. Her enthusiasm is adorable though, and it immediately dampens my initial disappointment.

"Oh, sorry," she apologies, and steps out of the room, "I'm keeping you."

I shake my head and laugh. "You should be an interior designer, instead of working for my brother," I offer, passing her I head straight for the shower.

"If only," I hear her say with a sigh, before I close the door behind me.

I take the shower cold, because the woman at the other side of the door has me as horny as hell. The temptation to go in there and pull her in here with me is driving me crazy. The image of her in just her underwear is still etched on my brain. But I have ten minutes to push down my erection and get my shit together.

As I step out of the shower, I think of soccer and baseball, anything to keep me distracted and my cock at half-mast. With a towel wrapped around my waist, I walk back into the bedroom. I manage to hide my surprise when I see that she's still in the room over by the window, taking in the view. The sun lights up her face, her dark hair shimmers and her expression is of someone who is in awe of what she sees. I walk toward her with determination, all my control smashed to pieces. When she hears me, she turns and I get up close. Her back hits the glass when she tries to take a step backwards. I lean into her, putting a hand at each side of her head, not once breaking the eye contact.

"I think you need to put some clothes on," she pants. Her chest rises and falls at a fast rate.

"I think you need to take some off," I counter, brushing her ponytail back over her shoulder, exposing her neck. I cup the side of her face with my hand, my thumb brushes the shell of her ear. She leans into my caress.

"They won't allow us in the dining room for breakfast in a state of undress."

"I think we should skip breakfast."

"I thought," her breath hitches when I lean in and replace my thumb with my lips, giving her a quick kiss, "you were hungry?"

"Who needs food?" I groan, desperate for more friction, as my cock nudges her stomach. "I'd rather feast on you." I push forward, pinning her harder against the window, until she's pressing against my chest. I move a hand to her hip, sliding it up until it skims the side of her breast. A soft moan escapes her lips and I move to capture her mouth with mine. Before our lips touch, the sound of a phone ringing stops us in our tracks.

Petra pulls her phone out of her pocket and holds it up in front of me.

"It's Kat," she pants, a little breathless. "I better get this." I give her a little space, but not too much, leaving my hand resting on her hip.

"Hi," she greets when she accepts the call. "Yes, yes, I'll be down in a minute." We keep eye contact as I listen to the one-sided conversation. "Did you, well I didn't hear you knocking. I must have been in the shower or something. Out of breath? A little I guess, but I was in the middle of some…" she stutters as my hand moves towards her ass. She bats it away then wags a finger at me, making me feel like the naughty boy that I so want to be right now. "…thing, some stretches, decided I need to get healthy. A little jogging on the spot." Her eyes go wide and her mouth gapes open. Shit! She really doesn't make it easy for me. "No, no, you don't have to come get me. I'm coming down now. I'm ready, starving actually, can't wait for pancakes and bacon. Mmm, yummy." I laugh and she slaps her palm over my mouth to muffle the sound, which makes me laugh more. "Of course, I'm on my own. Cade? Not seen him. Really? He must have left during the night. Yes, I'm on my way, bye, bye…" Finishing the call, she removes her hand from my mouth.

"I think we should go to breakfast, like now. Kat's already suspicious and when she's like that, she's like a super sleuth, and won't rest until she gets to the truth."

"That we spent the night together, in your bed? Is that such a bad thing?" I tease.

"Come on, Cade," she reprimands me. "It's the wedding

of my good friend and your brother. It just… looks bad."

"What if I like bad?" I move in close, our lips millimetres away from each other's.

"Not today, Cowboy," she says, pushing me away.

"Why do you keep calling me Cowboy?"

"Because you remind me of one."

"In what way?" I laugh. "I'm not wearing a Stetson; chaps and I don't own any spurs."

"You just do, okay?" She goes to walk past me, but I grab her arm and stop her.

"Explain."

"You know. Tall, muscular, good looking. Golden tan and dirty blond hair that looks like it's been touched on the tips by the sun."

"You think I'm good looking." I pull her towards me, and she falls against my chest. "We should skip breakfast. Let Kat come looking." I place my lips on her neck, right where I can feel the thumping of her pulse. "She doesn't know my room number, and by the time she finds out, you'll be so distracted, you won't even care." I lift my head and try to read her reaction.

"Cade." Her pupils are dilated, her lips open and pouty, and her face slightly flushed. I already know that her heart is racing. "I need to go."

"Okay," I relax my hold on her a little, but not enough for her to escape. "I'll let you go, but only if you agree to meet up with me later."

"I'm here with Kat. I can't disappear on her without some explanation." She tilts her head down, and I wonder where the confident, sassy Petra has gone.

"Don't worry." I stroke a finger along her jawline before using it to lift her chin up, so our eyes meet. "I'll arrange something. I'm sure Ben will help. Agreed?"

"Okay," she half smiles, confirming that she's still a little on edge.

"Good," I nod. "Do you want to go down now? It will be less obvious if we turn up separately."

"Yes please," her whole body becomes visibly more relaxed, as she grabs her purse from the bed, where she left it. I follow her through the living area to the main door, when she stops and turns to face me.

"I'll be down in a few minutes." As I step back from placing a small kiss on her forehead, I notice her eyes are still shut and her expression is soft, almost angelic. An image I want to keep. When her eyes do flutter open, she smiles at me, as if embarrassed at being caught. This woman has more to her than meets the eye.

Petra opens the door and steps outside.

"Cade," she turns to address me. "Thank you."

"What for?"

"Just… Thank you." She smiles sweetly as she walks towards the elevator.

I watch her until she's no longer in sight.

CHAPTER 5

Cade

I walk into the dining room about fifteen minutes later and immediately my eyes fall to Petra, who's already sitting at the table with Kat and Amy. She quickly glances my way, but it's fleeting, her attention turning back to the conversation.

Isaac and Ben are standing a few feet away, so I go to join them.

"Fucking hell brother, congratulations." Ben gives Isaac a man hug.

"Did we not do all this already, Ben, or are you getting all over emotional on us?" I titter.

"Amy's pregnant," Isaac announces. He has the biggest grin on his face and I can tell that he's one very happy man.

"Shit, man!" I can't miss the chance of busting his balls. "So that's why you married her?" Isaac's expression changes instantly.

"Amy only told me last night, you ass."

"Ball, chain and another kid on the way," I continue. "You're well and truly trapped, boy. This is for real buddy, no get out of jail free card this time." I say, referring to the staged marriage to my sister.

Isaac, although family to us, he's not blood. So, when our sister got pregnant to a low life who immediately ghosted her once he found out, without a second thought Isaac stepped up to save our family from shame. And although it was all a lie, he was nothing but a perfect father figure for Mikey. "You won't be able to get out of this one that easy." I pat him hard on the back. "Rather you than me, brother. You're well and truly pussy whipped this time."

"Fuck off, Cade." Isaac squares up to me.

"Isaac," Amy's voice suddenly breaks through. Isaac immediately turns to his new wife.

"See what I mean," I snigger.

Isaac storms out of the room. Amy gets up from her seat and walks toward me.

"Cade, sometimes you're an utter arsehole." She chastises, before leaving to following Isaac.

Ben looks at me and shakes his head before going to join the ladies at the table.

"What?" I laugh. "I've left my phone in my room. Order me a black coffee, Ben. I'll be back in a second."

Ben would have been calling me the pussy, if he'd have known that my phone was safely in my pocket but that I actually wanted to seek out Isaac, to apologise.

I find him in the reception area. Amy stands facing him,

looking up at him with adoration. Her hands resting against his chest as she speaks softly to him. The chemistry between them is electric.

"Hey!" I call as I walk towards them, my hands raised up in surrender. "I'm sorry. I was being an ass. I was only busting your balls man, but it was in poor taste."

"Too far, Cade. You took it too fucking far. Don't you ever disrespect Amy like that."

"Amy." I pull her away from Isaac and into a hug. "I'm so sorry. You are beautiful, kind, and incredibly sexy. I couldn't ask for a better person to take on my dick of a brother. We've been trying to get rid of him since Dad took pity on him and brought him into the family."

"Cade," Isaac grumbles out a warning.

"But I'm not sure if we should inflict his assholery on you," I know, I'm an ass, but this is what I do when it comes to Isaac. "It's not too late to back out, you know. I'm more than willing to take care of you," I give Amy an exaggerated wink, at which she tries her best to stifle her giggle.

"Fuck you," Isaac laughs, pulling Amy back into the confinements of his own arms. His temper now obviously quashed from Amy's affection, and the realisation that as far as an apology from me goes, this is as good as it gets.

"Come on, you two lovebirds. Let's go get some breakfast, I'm starving."

Petra

Kat is still interrogating me when Cade walks back

in, closely followed by Isaac and Amy. The heat of the previous confrontation seems to have diminished and the happy wedding aura slowly seeps back into the group.

Kat, being the type to rub it in, takes great pleasure in informing me that most of the other guests, that were staying overnight, have already had breakfast and gone. Some making their way home, others going out for the day and taking advantage of the Florida sun.

"I can understand Isaac and Amy wanting to hole up until late. They get to play the just married card, but what's your excuse?" Kat asks, still convinced that I was holding back vital information. I hate liars, but this isn't lying, is it? I'm just refusing to divulge my recent inappropriate and embarrassing behaviour. Although, I secretly wish that things had gone further, a lot further, whilst my backbone had been under the influence of a bottle and a half of champagne. Don't let those sparkles fool you, it's really the devil in a glass. With the way my head feels, Beelzebub is certainly taking the piss out of me this morning.

"The hangover from hell," I groan as I pop another pain killer, aware that having already taken two less than an hour ago, I shouldn't, really. Hell, if I'm going to get through today, I need a top up. I could go down the hair of the dog route, but I doubt my stomach could take it. Coffee and a round of toast are about as much as I'm willing to risk.

"So, ladies, what are your plans for the day?" Cade asks, taking the vacant seat next to me.

"We were going to drive over to Orlando and spend the day at one of the parks," Kat replies, before the question has even registered with me. The closeness of him is very distracting. "But looking at Petra, rollercoasters and screaming kids are off today's agenda."

"Huh?" I jump at the sound of my name.

"Ben and I are going out to Pierce Street Market if you would like to join us?"

"Are we?" Ben mutters. Cade gives him a 'shut up and go with it' look. "Yeah! They have some outstanding food stalls, and we could show you the beach, too. Best beach in Florida." He adds, immediately backing up his brother's impromptu plan.

"I don't know," I say, rubbing my stomach when it rolls, and not in a good way, at the mention of food. Cade's hand drops onto my knee and squeezes. Undoubtedly, to remind me of my previous promise.

"I think that's a great idea," Kat intervenes. "And some fresh air will do you good," she directs at me.

"Excellent," Cade expels over zealously, patting my leg before removing his hand. "Let's meet in the lobby, say, an hour?" I agree, even if a little less enthusiastically than the others. "It will be warm, so dress light. Oh, and flip-flops or sneakers as there will be a good amount of walking."

"Fuck me," I mumble under my breath, already marking up the day as a nightmare. Hot, sticky, walking? All I really want to do is go veg out at the side of the hotel pool, with a bucket of full sugar coke and my Kindle. I'm so not looking forward to this.

"Did you say something, Petra?" Cade raises his eyebrows at me. Not one, but two.

"Lucky me," I speak louder. "Can't wait." I try to make the words sound less sarcastic than I actually want it to, but it's like I'm on autopilot. It's just me.

"Good," he gives me a half smile. You know the kind that says, I know your game.

We all finish our breakfast around the same time and make our way back into the lobby.

Isaac and Amy have already done a disappearing act. It was probably for the best, because at one point, I'm sure that one of Isaac's hands had certainly not been sticking to table etiquette. By the expression on Amy's face, the way she was biting her lip and the flush to her cheeks, the addition to her conventional breakfast serving, had hit the spot.

Ben and Kat walked ahead towards the lifts, chatting away. I can sense Cade's presence, even before he's moved up close beside me. It's as if his masculine pheromones radiate off him like a… well heat from a radiator… at maximum temperature. Did someone switch off the air-con?

"For a minute, I thought you were going to bail on me," he accuses. His hand comes to rest at the hollow of my back.

"Steady on, Cowboy. I never break a promise, I just didn't expect it to be today."

"I'm not a patient guy. I believe that once an agreement is made, it should be dealt with quickly and efficiently."

"Is that so? Well, I'm hardly going to argue with you, am I now? Mister Lawyer Man."

"Glad you see things my way," he chuckles. I huff at him and his arrogance. "Oh, and while we are on the subject of promises," his hand slips to my hip, pulling me closer to his side as his mouth hovers over my ear. "Be careful," he warns. "You should make sure I'm not around when you mumble 'fuck me' because, like I said before, I don't need asking twice." I swear he nips my ear with his teeth before finishing with, "And that is a promise."

He picks up his pace, catching up with Kat and Ben as they step into the lift. He turns to watch me as I stand, in rigid shock, on the spot. His eyes are fixed securely on my face, and I'm sure as eggs are eggs, my mouth is open, face glowing red with embarrassment, my bottom jaw not far from hitting the floor.

"Earth to Petra, earth to Petra," Kat sniggers. I realise I must look like the Walking Dead, as I seem to have lost the ability to blink. "Are you coming or what?"

I snap out of it, step into the lift and spin my back to Cade, unable to cope under his scrutiny. Kat and Ben chatter away, occasionally Cade adding a few words to the conversation. The whole time I sense the heat of his eyes on my back, my body bubbles as his promised words run riot in my head.

Be careful.

Don't need asking twice.

That's a promise.

I hope to God, I'm not thinking out loud as 'Fuck me, fuck me, fuck me,' keeps jumping in there too. In my own voice. Mashing up with his deep tones.

How the hell am I going to get through today?

CHAPTER 6

Cade

Both Ben and I are waiting in the lobby. As yet, there's no sign of Petra or Kat.

"So, what's going on, brother?" Ben wiggles his eyebrows at me, which is code for, did you get laid last night?

"Give me some credit, Ben," I grumble. "She was drunk."

"Since when has that stopped you?" he sniggers. "Wait a minute. That could only mean one thing. Damn it, Cade. I was right, you do like her."

"Back the fuck off, asshole." I'm about to set him straight about what had actually happened when the elevator pings. "Not another word Ben, you ruin this for me and I'll feed your cock to an alligator, while the rest of you is still attached."

"Chill, man," he huffs and I elbow him in the ribs for good measure. "Ouch! Jesus, look at those legs!"

Ben is referring to Kat and I'm sure she looks good, but my eyes instantly gravitate to Petra.

The bright yellow, tank top she's wearing is tight, almost like a second skin. The rounded neck scoops low and barely covers her bra, giving a splendid view of the peaks of her breasts. Vintage denim, hi-rise shorts with frayed edges and tears make her legs seem longer than I last remember them. Her skin, that soft, smooth olive skin brings flash backs of how perfect it felt against my fingertips.. The thought of my hands touching her, pulling her legs until they're wrapped around my neck, while I bury my...

Fortunately, the two girls are busy talking amongst themselves, and Ben only has eyes for Kat. I don't think anyone notices when I push my hardened dick to a less uncomfortable position as inconspicuously as I possibly can, given the circumstances.

"Ready to go, ladies?" I ask once I'd coughed and cleared my throat.

"Yes, we are. Aren't we Petra?" Kat side bumps her friend.

"Saddle up, Cowboy," Petra stands firm, her hands on her hips. "Let's haul ass."

"Cowboy?" Ben looks at me, confused. "Why is she calling you Cowboy?"

***

The drive from the hotel to the market only takes a

few minutes. We park the car nearby and walk along Drew Street towards where the market is held, here in Clearwater. The Pierce Street Market is located under the Memorial Causeway Bridge, next to the harbour marina.

"Wow!" Petra gasps. "What a view." Her face alight with amazement.

Even for me, having seen it many times, it still takes my breath away. The huge white pillars of the bridge against the clear blue sky, peppered with palm trees, are outstanding. Every colour of the rainbow visible around the various vendor stalls. Whether it be flowers, fabrics, handmade soaps, candles, pottery and crafts, it's a vision to be seen.

The aromatics are so tempting. A mix of all the original foods from around the globe has your taste buds jumping to attention and your mouth salivating, eager to taste the variety of international cuisine.

Ben and Kat gain some distance from us as they walk upfront, still talking away, both hardly aware of their surroundings. Kat stops now and again, for a quick look at some of the stalls selling food items, but otherwise she seems to be happy with Ben's company.

Petra, on the other hand, stops at most of the tables, checking out the items for sale with a new found enthusiasm.

"Cade," she shouts as she grabs my hand and pulls me towards one vendor. "Look at these." I miss her touch when she lets go to pick up a bright pink bar of soap. Bringing it up to her nose, she breathes in the fragrance. "Mmm, smell it," she says, holding it up towards me. I take advantage of the opportunity to catch her hand again, bringing it towards my nose, as I sniff the bar. I hold on longer than necessary, but shoot me. I'm loving it.

"Strawberry and vanilla."

"You know what it is?" she questions me.

"Of course," I put on my most serious face. "Not really," I confess, and point to the label at the side of identical soaps stacked on the table.

"Arsehole," she laughs and smiles, and the sun is no longer the brightest thing I've ever seen.

"That," I whisper. Standing close, I look down at her upturned face, her hand still firmly in mine.

"What?" she whispers back.

"Your smile." I bring my free hand up to her face, holding it in place, to stop her from turning away. "Now that is an amazing view." I lean forward, with the intention to steal a kiss. Needing to have the softness of her lips against my own, only to be interrupted by my asshole of a brother.

"Cade," Ben shouts, and I reluctantly step back, breaking all connections. I do, however, notice the flash of disappointment that sweeps across Petra's face.

"What's up, brother?"

"You're too slow, man. We both need a drink."

"Go to Lucky's on Cleveland Street, we'll catch you up." I shout back at him. Ben gives me the thumbs up before jogging back to where Kat is and they both turn and walk away.

"I think my brother has the hots for your girlfriend."

"I think it might be reciprocated," she laughs hard.

"What's so funny?"

"Nothing really, it's just calling her my girlfriend," she waves her hand at me, trying to brush it off, but still laughing. "It sounds weird, that's all. Back home a girlfriend is a partner."

"But she's a girl, and she's your friend, so, girlfriend."

"True, but we tend to go with friend." I frown at her and she instantly responds to it. "Think of it this way, you wouldn't call your mate your boyfriend, would you? Unless you were in a same sex relationship."

"I guess, but then why call them mate?" I counter. "That gives the impression that you're having sex as in mating."

"Touché. I can't argue with that," she concedes.

Petra decides to purchase a bar of the strawberry and vanilla soap, but I intervene, adding two or three more bars of the different fragrances, before handing a fifty-dollar bill to the vendor.

"Cade," she says, pushing my hand away and holding out her own bills.

"Please, let me," I push my hand further forward, my height giving me the advantage.

"I can pay for my own things," she scowls at me. I think it's meant to be scary, but it's actually kind of cute. "I don't like being indebted to anyone."

"It's a gift, Petra. Nothing more, nothing less." Hooking my finger through the gift bag straps, I hold it out to her. "A gift," I clarify.

"Okay," she nods at me, her sass subsiding. "Thank you, Cade."

"You can make it up to me later." Her shoulders go back and her height increase a few inches as she rears up at me. "Joke; I'm joking." I laugh.

"You little shit!" she bats my arm and I rub the area,

making out that it hurt.

"Ouch!" I drape my arm around her shoulder. "Come on, let's go get that drink."

Petra

After drinks, we take a walk around the marina. Some of the boats anchored are bigger than my place in Bath. The quality and luxury of them shouts big money, the cost of mooring here in itself, must be mega bucks.

I lean up against the white painted railing, looking at a sizeable white craft with a large deck at the back and a table of eight chairs laid out. Plush cushions are scattered around a deep seating area that runs around the edge. The words 'Jack The Lads' written in bold blue letters across the stern.

"Mmm, I can imagine sitting there eating fresh grilled fish, while drinking a glass of crisp white Sauvignon. Out there," I point and look out to sea, "watching the sun go down."

"You should do it," Cade says, leaning into me.

"The fish and wine I can handle, but the boat. Maybe one day, when I've won the lottery." I let out a deep sigh. "Sorry, stupid daydreams."

"There's nothing wrong with dreaming, Petra." I can sense his eyes on me, so I turn to meet them. "Rich, poor, young, old; we all need something to wish for."

"I'm finding it really hard figuring you out, Cowboy."

"I'm not a complicated man, Petra. What you see is what you get."

"But that's it. I'm never sure what I'm going to see next."

He shrugs his shoulders, as if not sure what to say to that.

Ben and Kat seem to appear from out of nowhere and suggest we go back to the car so we can drive across the bridge to Clearwater Beach.

If Clearwater Beach was in a tin, the name on the label would be exactly what you'd get. Clean, aquamarine water laps at the white gold sand. Spotlessly clean, stretching farther than the eye can see, spectacular in every way.

I slip off one of my flip-flops, and put my foot onto the hot sand, only to pull it straight back off and replace it in the flip-flop.

"Shit, that's hot," I gasp.

"If you walk in the water, the sand will be cooler there," Cade offers.

"No, it's okay. I'm good." I can see that, yet again, Kat and Ben are walking far out in front. "Either I've pissed Kat off, or Ben doesn't like me very much?"

"It's not that," Cade laughs. "Ben likes everyone. He got Mum's easy-going attitude."

"Then why do I get the impression that he's avoiding me? Or is he avoiding you?"

"He's not avoiding anyone, he's just..."

"Ahh," I laugh. "Let me guess. It's a brother thing, isn't it? If one of you is with a girl, you give them some space."

"Only if we know they really like them."

"Wow, does he really like her then?"

"I wouldn't know."

"Then why?" I look at the pair of them off in the distance, then look back at Cade.

"It works both ways, Petra," he says softly.

"Oh!" I'm not sure what to say, but for some reason, I have the need to clarify. "So, what you're saying is…"

"That Ben is giving me space." He puts his arm around my waist and spins me so I'm facing him.

"But what would make him think you like me?" I ask, a little breathless.

"Because I told him I did."

"Oh!" This time I am gob smacked.

"Have dinner with me tonight, just you and me?"

"What about Kat? I can't ditch her."

"Well, at least that wasn't a flat-out no." He pulls me a little closer, his mouth mere millimetres from my own. "I'm sure that Ben will be only too happy to entertain Kat for the night. Look at them, they're like best buddies."

"We could all go out together?" I offer, the flutter of nerves take flight in my belly. Or was it his closeness that was getting me all worked up?

"Not happening," he murmurs against my mouth. "I want you all to myself." My knees nearly buckle when his lips touch mine, softly at first, but when he increases the pressure, a soft moan resonates from deep within me. He breaks the kiss and asks again. "Dinner, you and me?"

"Okay, but do you think we could get a snack or something now, because I'm starving."

"Damn!" His face suddenly full of concern. "I'm not looking after you very well, am I?"

I see another side to Cade, when he starts to flap about

finding a restaurant. I convince him that a sandwich, from one of the beach takeout's, is more than enough. In fact, we end up sharing, neither of us wanting to eat too much and spoil our dinner later. Ben and Kat easily polish off one each.

On the way back to the car, Cade and Ben have both Kat and me in stitches, once again telling tales about each other, and their childhood antics. All in all, it's been a great day and so much more fun than vegging in the sun; the stories on my Kindle ain't going nowhere either.

CHAPTER 7

Petra

Considering Kat is meant to be meeting Ben in under an hour, I can't seem to get her to leave.

When we get back, she follows me to my room, determination set on her face. Even before the click of the door latch closing, the interrogation starts.

"Right, what happened last night?" she asks, placing her back firmly against the door.

"Before or after I propositioned Cade?"

"No way! You were fast asleep when I left." Kat moves to sit on the edge of the bed. "Tell me he took you up on your offer?"

"Nope, he's actually quite the gentleman." I sigh. "We kissed."

"Oooo, we have progress." Kat claps her hands together.

"But then I was sick."

"Oh, not good."

"All down his shirt."

"Eek! Is that when he left?"

"No, on the contrary, like I said before, he was the perfect gentleman, or carer; not sure which, really. He held my hair, wiped my face, and tucked me up in bed."

"What aren't you telling me?" she looks at me suspiciously. "You know I won't give up until I know everything."

"I need to shower," I say, walking into the bathroom to avoid having to answer.

"You can run, but you can't hide," she shouts as I turn the water on.

Kat makes me jump when she shouts from the other side of the door. "He stopped the night, didn't he?"

"You don't know that."

"I think I do." She pushes open the door and puts her head around. "I can understand the cufflinks, seen as you spewed your guts up all over him, but this?" She waves Cade's watch from side to side in front of her face. "Not so easy to explain."

"Bloody hell, Poirot," I squeal, as I try to cover my nakedness.

"Come on, I've seen you naked before." She waves my sudden shyness away. With a hand towel, she covers the toilet seat and sits. "Get in the shower then. Oh, for God's sake," she spins on her bottom and puts her back to me. "Now tell me, did you at least have morning sex?"

***

By the time Kat leaves after giving me an ear bashing, telling me to get a pair of balls. I'm running late. Yes, I corrected her, and pointed out the saying is to grow a pair, but she said, in my case I definitely need to get a man and grab his pair.

I'm due to meet Cade in the lobby in ten minutes, but I'm still undecided as to what to wear. The cat suit I wore at the wedding is out because, well, you wouldn't wear the same thing twice, would you? My options are limited, as I packed more for casual days out and lazy sunbathing, rather than nights out with the hottest guy that's looked at me in months. Technically, that's only a half-truth but he's the only guy I've let get this close in a long time.

Yes, I flirt and come across as a sassy, confident woman, but as soon as it comes to the crunch, when they want to get hands on, I'm the fastest wall builder ever to come out of Slovakia.

In short. I bottle it.

Why? Because I'm scared shitless that history will repeat itself. That I'll end up on what I think is the road to happiness, only to find that it leads me to an emotional nightmare. Again.

A knock on the door brings me out of my depressing train of thought. Still not dressed, I grab the bathrobe and pull it around me. When I open the door, I find Cade.

What can I say?

Man in a suit.

Cut perfectly to honour his physique and a crisp white

shirt open at the neck. He has a body to die for and a face that you'd unashamedly want to lick.

Girl down!

"You're late." The way his eyes slowly move down my body, his gaze so intense, has me checking that I haven't flipped, and I do have the robe on. He makes me feel naked. Do I want to be naked?

"I'm sorry. Blame Kat. Her interrogation is very thorough, to say the least. By the way, your watch and cufflinks are on the bedside cabinet."

"Ah!" Cade walks over and picks them up. "That explains why you got the interrogation. Sorry. It can't have been that bad, surely?"

"She was one step away from the thumbscrews. So, forgive me if I ruined your bad boy reputation by telling her you had been nothing but the perfect gentleman."

"Damn," he laughs. "I think you better get dressed before I do something that proves that I'm not always a gentleman. I'm guessing that under that robe you're naked and that is too much of a temptation."

I grab the first dress I can lay my hands on, quickly adding the underwear that I'd already chosen, thankfully one with multi-straps, and scoot into the bathroom to dress.

I make it quick, well as quick as I can, but when trying to make the strap of the bra go around my neck, it won't go long enough. I end up with my chin to my chest, making it look like I'm only interested in my own cleavage. Decision made; I go for the strapless option. Braless is not even in the equation, as the fabric of the dress is the type that would mould to your nipples at the first sign of a breeze. The black halter neck dress is fitted at the top, but then flares out from the waist and, although quite plain, the neckline gives it a 1950s vibe. I fluff my hair from underneath, then smooth down the top. A coat of red lippy and I'm ready.

Stepping back into the room, the swish of the door has Cade looking up from his mobile phone that is firmly in his hand.

He doesn't say a word, only slips his phone into his pocket, and walks towards me with an air of sheer determination. The heat of his gaze, as it sweeps across my body, has my heart racing. When he stands before me, the intensity in his eyes has me catching my breath.

"You are stunning," he murmurs, as he traces his index finger across my jaw line. I can't control the shiver that runs through me from his touch, nor the pounding pulse that beats between my legs. I'm not sure if the quaking of my body is because of my arousal or the triggering of my fears.

When his gaze falls to my lips, I'm convinced he's going to kiss me, but I'm hit with a bout of disappointment when he takes a step back.

"I think we better go."

"I'm sorry, are we going to be late for a reservation?" I say, a little breathless.

"A little, but I'm more concerned that if we don't go now, we might not get there at all."

"Oh, right, let me get my shoes and bag." Tonight, already has me shitting myself. If I'm going to get a pair of balls, rather than grow a pair, I need some alcoholic assistance.

Cade

Hell, this woman is gorgeous. The way her dress moulds to her upper body does everything to showcase her tits and slender waist. The flare of the skirt does two things. It emphasises her perfect hour-glass figure and has me imagining what the underwear, I saw her snatch up earlier, would look like on her glorious body.

I was so damn close to kissing her, but when I saw something in her eyes that bordered on fear, I backed off. Something has her spooked.

The car I've arranged to drive us to the restaurant waits for us as we step outside the hotel. The journey isn't long, and the conversation flows. However, the temptation of being so close to her in such a confined space is torture. But my determination not to fuck this up is enough to keep me in control.

The restaurant is small, intimate and expensive, but the food is to die for and worth every dollar. Spending the evening with Petra is worth a million dollars.

We eat, we drink and we laugh a lot. It's easy and comfortable. Although I'm only just getting to know her, it's so relaxed, it's like I've known her for years. I find myself wanting to know everything about her.

When the server delivers the check, disappointment hits me, as I realise that the night is nearly over.

On our return to the hotel, I declare that one last drink in the hotel bar is a must and thankfully; she agrees. I don't want today to end, but when I notice her trying to stifle a yawn, I know that It's pure selfishness on my part.

"On second thoughts, why don't we skip that drink, you look beat."

"I'm fine," she flat out yawns this time, unable to hide it even behind her hand. "Sorry."

"No, I'm sorry," I say, taking her delicate hand in mine, holding it close to my chest. "It's been a long day. Let me walk you to your room."

"Okay," she sighs, and I wonder if I'm not the only one who doesn't want to call it a night.

Even the elevator seems to be against me, when the doors open as soon as I press the button. I let Petra walk in first and follow close behind her. The door closes, leaving just the two of us in the private confinements of the carriage. I slide my hands on her hips and bring her against me. With her head against my chest, she slides her arms around my waist, hugging me back. I feel the heat of her body as she relaxes and moulds against me.

Tilting her head back, she looks up at me. Her words come out soft and sleepy, yet clearly full of sincerity. "Thank you for today. I've had a wonderful time."

I respond by pulling her even tighter to me. "Believe me, it's been an absolute pleasure." Our mouths are close, so close that if she puckers her lips the tiniest amount, they'll touch. An internal fight goes on within me. Should I kiss her? I want to kiss her. But I don't want to see that fear that I saw earlier. Before I even get the chance to decide, the elevator door opens, and the moment is lost.

We walk together, my arm across her shoulders, her arm around my waist, until we get to her door. Facing each other, we lock eyes, each of us waiting for the other to say something. Both of us not wanting to be the one to make that final move.

"Would you like a coffee? I have a machine in my room." She points a finger over her shoulder. "I could really do with a coffee."

"Sure, I think a coffee would be nice."

"Great stuff." As she turns, she gets the key card from her bag and swipes it. After three attempts with shaky hands, I put mine around hers to hold it steady. The light flicks from red to green and I push the door open.

"Thank you," she murmurs and drops her bag onto the narrow cabinet that stands inside the entrance. "I'll go check there's enough water in the machine. What would you like? I think it does latte…" I grab her wrist and spin her around to face me. I take a step forward, so she's trapped against the cabinet, "or maybe you'd prefer an Americano." I stare deep into her eyes, trying to read her. "Espresso?"

"You." I say with conviction, I don't want to hold back any longer. "I want you." I let my hand caress the side of her face. My thumb traces the line of her chin before skimming over her bottom lip. "I want to kiss you, touch every inch of you. But do you want it too?" When my thumb sweeps over her bottom lip again, she captures it with her teeth, sucking it into her mouth. I groan out my approval, taking it as a clear sign for me to make my move. I'm conflicted though, because her eyes tell me a different story. She releases my thumb, and it slides slowly from her mouth. I spread the saliva that coats the pad, across her bottom lip before teasing it down, exposing the tip of her pink tongue. With our faces so close, I whisper my question into her open mouth.

"What are you scared of, Petra?"

Petra

What are you scared of? His words ricochet around my head like a ball in a pinball machine. What aren't I afraid of? I'm afraid of letting go, taking that step, falling in too deep. Losing control of myself, my life, giving away what I've only just regained. Yet I know that this is nothing serious. For all intents and purposes, it's a one-night stand. Others do it, why not me? He's hot, he's off the chart sexy, and to be honest, I'm sick of walking away when what I really need is a good hard fucking. I need to grab my girly bits and do this.

"Petra?" The sound of Cade's deep lust laced voice snaps me into deciding. I suck in a deep breath. Cade removes his hands and takes a step back, away from me. "I'll go."

"The fuck you will," I pant out. Popping up on my tiptoes, I grip each side of his head, pulling his face down and into my kiss. A deep growl echoes in his throat at the same time as he grabs my thighs, lifts, and plonks me down onto the cabinet. My arse is up against the wall, but with the unit only being narrow, the only thing stopping me from toppling forward is Cade's up and close hard body. Our kisses become frenzied, as if we both want to eat the living daylights out of each other. It suddenly occurs to me that if he puts this much into a kiss, then the sex is going to be manic. I grip onto the hair at the back of his neck and pull, while in my head I chant to myself, 'Don't panic.'

Cade's hands go behind my neck, quickly unfastening the catch that holds together the halter neck. The straps slide down, but the pressure of Cade's body keeping me in place stops the fabric from falling further and exposing my bra. He breaks the kiss, only to run the tip of his tongue from my bottom lip down until he reaches the small hollow at my throat. He grazes along my collarbone with his teeth, when he gets to my shoulder he nips the skin, then rubs his lips against the now tender spot.

I'm already wet between my legs. My body alight with arousal, screaming for more, my pussy pulsates in anticipation of what it so desperately needs.

His mouth stays firmly against my skin when he slides his hands between the hardwood surface and my arse, lifting me up. I cling onto his hard shoulders, and wrap my legs around his waist. I hook my feet together to strengthen my hold on him.

"What are you doing?" I ask breathlessly when he pulls me away from the wall.

"Fuck, Petra, you're driving me crazy." His lips cover mine again. Tongues moving together, with a hint of urgency and determination. He carries me over to the foot of the bed; slowly releases his hold and I slide down his body. I cling to him, not wanting to break the kiss, not wanting to let him go. Not wanting this to stop.

He pulls away and takes a few steps backwards, leaving me standing alone. My lips seem to be swollen, but I don't care. If by the end of the night they fell off, I wouldn't give a shit, it would be worth every single kiss.

He grabs a chair and places it in the centre of the room, only a few feet away from where I stand. Once he takes the seat, he watches me, his pupils so dilated that the blue of his iris is almost non-existent.

"Take off your clothes." His voice is low and harsh, but not with anger. With lust. My hands move at speed, clumsily trying to get to the little side zip of my dress. "Slowly," he orders.

"Why?" I ask. It's not that I don't want to, I'm not sure if I can do it without looking a total tit. I know I can come across as a bit of a minx, but now that I'm under the spotlight, so to speak, I'm more likely to look clumsy rather than sexy. "It's not like you haven't already seen me in my underwear."

"I want to watch as you …" he points at me with his index finger, "show yourself to me. I want you to strip for me."

An uncontrollable shiver shoots down my spine. His words have me wondering if there's a darker, dominant side to Cade. It rattles my nerves a bit. Cracks appear in my mind as doubt seeps in. But my inner curiosity also wants to find out how deep Cade's sexual preferences go. So, I take the metal zip tag at the side of my dress and slide it down slowly. When it reaches my waist, it takes a little more force to get past the seam, but when it does, the garment becomes undone and floats to the floor, leaving me standing in my underwear.

The cut of the black lace knickers is my preferred style. Resting softly at the hip, the side slightly higher with a little v indent that helps make my legs look longer than they actually are. The bra, well, that cost me an arm and a leg, but then, you need to spend the cash if you want one that stays in place when you remove the straps. Even though I say it myself, it makes my boobs look amazing. The cup is low enough to accentuate the soft domes. When I look down, I see the tiniest edge of my areola showing. My fingers twitch, wanting to hitch up the bra and reposition, but I force myself to leave it be. I stand still, my arms laid across my stomach, as I fidget at being so exposed.

"I'm waiting." Cade's words are sharp, and I know it's make or break. Either I tell him to leave and that this is a mistake, or I take that step, the step that will break through the invisible shield that I'm cocooned in.

I take a deep breath and let my arms fall loosely to my side. Another deep breath and I unhook my bra with one hand, while still holding the cups in place with my forearm. Gradually sliding the bra away, I expose my breasts. The coolness of the air conditioning wafts across my already hardened nipples, causing me to take a sudden intake of breath and another uncontrollable shiver. I'm not cold; if anything, I'm hot with both arousal and want.

With the palms of my hands flat against my hips, I slide them down, my fingers going under each side of my knickers. As my hands move lower, so does the lace fabric that is covering the last bit of my vulnerability. Once they get past my upper thighs, they freefall to the floor. The cheap costume jewellery around my neck and wrist, along with the simple cubic zirconia earring studs, are all that are left on my body. I stand there naked, and the way Cade looks at me makes me feel like I'm a rare diamond. Scratch that. More like a rare steak, and he's been out on the ranch, breaking horses, a real hungry cowboy.

"Turn around and face the bed." His voice is deep and demanding, so with little hesitation, I do as he asks.

The fast and loud beating of my heart is all I can hear, so when his arms come around my body, each hand covering a breast, I jump.

"You've surprised me, Petra." His mouth is close to my ear, his words are not much more than a whisper, but clear and precise.

"In a good or bad way?" I question.

"Good. Oh baby, most definitely good." His touch is soft and warm as he fondles my breasts. "When I saw the fear in your eyes earlier, the hesitation just now, I didn't think you would follow my direction." He pinches both nipples hard, and I let out a whimper. "Now I know you're ready, I get to play."

Although not blindfolded, I can't see what he's doing behind my back. But I feel it.

His mouth against my skin as it follows the line of my backbone, punctuated with the sporadic flick of his wet tongue. When he gets past my shoulder blades, he releases my breasts, moving his hands to my hips. I know he must have dropped to his knees, because his mouth continues the trail all the way to the crease of my bum. My arse cheeks get the same attention that my boobs are now missing, but instead of a pinch, it's a nip of what most definitely are his teeth. I squeal, my body instantly trying to pull forward, but his firm grip of my hips stops me from escaping.

"Mmm," he murmurs from behind me. One hand leaves

my hip, moving to my arse, as his finger follows the line of my bum crease. "You have the perfect ass." I now feel his hot, wet mouth as his tongue pushes between the crack. I realise that I'm holding my breath, unsure on how this makes me feel. Part of me wants him to go no further, yet I'm unable to ignore the rush of excitement that courses through my veins. Before I get the chance to come to terms with my mixed emotions, his mouth leaves my skin. I go to turn, but he stops my movement with his firm hands. "Stay," he commands.

I hear and sense him moving behind me, and I open my mouth to say the first words that come into my head. "What's coming next?"

"You, hopefully."

Quivering lady lips! The way he speaks in his deep American accent is as seductive as fuck. If I was a bloke, I'd have the biggest, solid boner, ever.

Skin; I have his glorious naked skin covering the whole of my back.

Woah now! Talk about boners. That's some major man meat prodding at my back. His arms come around me, taking hold of my breasts once again, while his mouth falls to my neck, kissing, sucking, his teeth nip at the skin. A squeeze, a pinch, a roll of each nipple has my body highly charged. When his hand moves over my stomach, continuing further down, I breathe in. As his fingers slip between my legs, to stroke my pussy, I hold that breath. When the tip of his fingers breach the lips and stroke right over my already awakened clit, my exhale comes out with a strangled scream as my orgasm explodes.

"Well, that didn't take long." You can hear the element of surprise in his voice.

"I'm sorry," I reply with a quiet giggle of embarrassment.

"Don't be sorry," he dips his finger inside me. "See how wet you are for me, Petra." Adding another finger, he dips in and out, spreading the wetness around. "And we've only just got started." His other hand joins in on the action. While two or three fingers pump in and out of me, the other hand is teasing my clit, circling and stroking.

My skin is hot, and sensitive, electrically charged. Every inch of me on high alert and already speeding towards another climax. It's too much, too quick and I can't take it. I'm about to push his probing hands away, when I'm consumed with an even harder hitting orgasm. His hands are relentless, still moving, still caressing as I ride it out, his name spilling from my lips amongst other things.

"Cade, stop, please stop, I can't take anymore," I pant out. Removing his fingers, he turns me to face him. I watch, in my orgasmic hazed vision, as he puts the same two fingers into his mouth and sucks them clean.

"Mmm! How can I stop, when you taste so good?" With a hard kiss, he slips his tongue into my mouth, the subtle saltiness coating my taste buds. "I think you can take a little more," he growls. Lifting me, he lays me down on the bed and nips at my left nipple with his teeth, before he takes position between my legs. When his breath hits the wetness, the area already swollen and sensitive to the slightest touch, my hips tilt towards him. My head might be reluctant, but my traitorous body wants more.

I almost scream out when his mouth covers the lips of

my pussy. The flat of his tongue slides across the seam and I whimper. When the tip of his tongue swipes across my swollen nub, I cry out unashamedly. He sucks and licks my clit like it's a Chupa Chups lolly, softly at first but then building the intensity, as if desperate to taste more. His nose rubs from side to side against my skin, his mouth doing the same as he flicks my clit. Again, I feel my arousal building, and it astounds me. Don't get me wrong, I've had a double before. I was allowed to come first, but only because they wanted me ready for what they wanted to do. On the odd occasion, I'd hit another orgasm by the time the other party got their own release. Most of the time, not. Never have I had this much attention, purely for my gratification only. Cade's touch can be so gentle, but then borders on painful when he nips and sucks hard. And it's the latter that has me racing at speed towards yet another euphoric state of ecstasy.

Cade

She looks fucking stunning, laid out on the bed, legs spread, full breasts, nipples hard and areola a shade of dusky pink. Lips slightly apart, her tits bounce erratically as she tries to regain a steady breathing rhythm. Hair fanned out around her head, her skin flush and glowing. With her arm flung over her eyes and her natural beauty, she reminds me of a movie starlet from the 1940s.

Her legs clamped against my head, when she came hard from my mouth, but I had slowly coaxed them apart, stroking her skin at her thigh until her body relaxed. The taste of her was incredible. I couldn't get enough and had taken full advantage of what she gave.

I kneel between her legs, a hand on each side of her shoulders as I lower myself, until I'm hovering mere centimetres from her, but not quite touching. I tilt my hips, so the tip of my cock just rests on her exposed pussy. It's swollen, the skin a darker shade of pink, almost red from her arousal. I let the swollen head of my cock push gently against the hood of her clit. Petra softly moans as she pushes back against me, looking to increase the pressure.

After running my cock down near to her asshole and back, I place it at the opening of her pussy and slowly push in. God, she's so warm and wet. I want to ram into the hilt, but I grit my teeth and harness my need to go in hard. Her cunt is tight, but adjusts to take me, and I'm all the way in. The sensation of her wrapped around my dick cock is driving me crazy. It is more than good. It's mind-blowing.

My movements are slow and precise. I come nearly all the way out, before I push all the way back in again. I groan out. I can't help it. She's like no other woman. I don't know what makes her stand out from all the rest, but she does. With her, it feels different, intoxicating.

As I'm on an outward thrust, struggling to keep things on the slow, she grabs my shoulders, her fingers grasping at the hard muscle, and pulls herself up to a half sitting position. "Fuck me!" she growls, almost like a possessed woman. "Fuck me, Cade."

I don't hesitate.

I drive in hard, causing her to dig her nails in deep.

"Yes!" she groans, as her head falls back, "Yes. Yes." Her moans of appreciation come rapidly along with my thrusts. "Ride me, Cowboy," she hollers as I begin to speed towards my release. I want to come, but I don't want this to stop.

I know it's pointless, trying to hold off any longer. "I'm going to come, Petra," I put my hand between us, finding her clit and flick it. "Come with me."

We come together, and it's noisy, hot and incredible. I can't describe how the sensation of her pussy, gripping my cock, as she matched the rhythm of my thrust, took me to a fresh experience.

I roll to her side. The only sound to be heard is the panting as we both try to catch our breath.

Through the haze of the moment, reality hits me.

"Fuck!" I growl. "We didn't use a rubber. Petra, I'm sorry."

"Shit, shit, shit." She covers her face with her hands. "Are you clean?" she hisses between her fingers. "I'm on the pill, but…"

"I've never done that before, well once, but that was back when I was a stupid, irresponsible teenager." I pull her hands away from her face and look her straight in the eye. "My last medical tested me clean. I won't lie and tell you I haven't been with other women, but I promise you, I used protection every goddamn time."

"Okay, okay," she breathes out a sigh of relief. "So, we're okay."

"Are we okay?" I hated asking but…

"Trust me, we're good." I raise an eyebrow in question.

"I'm clean." She reiterates.

I don't give in that easily. Hell, I'm curious how she can be so sure. I keep eye contact and eventually she breaks.

"Okay, so you want the gory details?" Pushing herself up, she flips back the bedsheets. Sitting crossed legged near the head of the bed, leaning against the board, she pulls the cotton sheet around herself, covering her nakedness. "When I found out my partner of two years had been sleeping around pretty much most of the time we'd been together, I dumped him and got checked out. Fortunately, the cheating bastard hadn't passed anything on from the skanky tarts he'd been shagging."

"And since then, you've used protection?"

"Erm!" she averts her eyes, "Something like that." Nervously pleating the edge of the sheet with her fingers, she doesn't realise that she's giving me a peek at her pink nipple. I know I've just had her, but it's enough to get me hard again.

"Something like what?" I ask, reluctantly averting my gaze from her perfect tits.

"Your-themm-firmmn-bein-wit," she mumbles. She's holding her head down as if in shame. I can't have that. I tilt her chin up gently with my index finger and dip my head until she can't avoid the connection.

"I'm the first man you've been with?" I recite her words back to her. She tugs away from me, and makes to move from the bed, but I catch her and pull her back into my arms. "Don't do that, Petra."

"Do what?" she snaps back.

"Don't run away from me." Her body is stiff and taut

with annoyance. "I'm honoured."

"Don't take the piss, Cade." Wiggling within my embrace, she tries again to get free.

"Petra, stop." I bark. Her eyes, now wide, instantly find mine. I realise the harshness of my voice has only turned her anger into fear. "Please, stop fighting me," I say softly. "You are a beautiful woman, and your body, well, it's something else. Do you realise how sexy you are?" I feel her body start to relax against me and I loosen my hold. I hold her chin between my finger and thumb, and place a delicate kiss on her soft lips. "I'm truly honoured that you let me spend this time with you. Now, it's getting late, maybe I should go?" I feel like a bit of a jerk to cut and run, but I must give her the option.

She pulls away from me, nods her head and slides fully under the covers, curling up into the foetal position.

"Okay." I lean into her and place my lips on her forehead. I hold them against her skin, not wanting to walk away, but I do.

I gather my clothes together, laying them at the bottom of the bed while I dress. With my pants on and my shirt pulled loosely around my chest, I sling my jacket over my shoulder and slip on my shoes.

"Goodnight, sweet Petra," I murmur, not sure if she's awake. Then I turn and walk towards the door.

"Don't go," I hear, but I'm not sure if it's just my wishful thinking.

"Please stay," I hear her say clearly and decisively.

I walk to the side of the bed nearest to her. I kick off my shoes, drop my jacket to the floor, tug off my shirt, and step out of my pants.

“Scoot over, pretty little lady,” I say in an exaggerated Texan accent. “Y’all need to make room for this cowboy.”

CHAPTER 8

Petra

I can't ever remember waking up with a man in my bed, and feeling like this.

Cade is big, strong, and commanding. I feel nothing but safe as I lounge across his body. My head rests on his perfectly toned chest, his arms wrapped around my body. Cade is 100% top shelf eye candy and although a little cocky at times, more than once, I've seen a softer side to him.

If only it wasn't short term, a holiday romance. If this is indeed the genuine Cade, and not some play acting to get me into bed. I smile to myself. If it is, his plan just worked. Anyway, what does it matter? In a couple of days, I'll be flying back home, the holiday fling over, exactly what I needed to put some cracks in the wall that I've built around myself.

No longer will I let the memory of being suppressed, controlled, and demoralised by that man consume me. Things can be different. I can be in control of my life choices. I can be me.

"Hey!" Cade's sleep muffled voice breaks through my head ramblings. "Good morning." He hugs me tighter, nuzzling my neck as he kisses the pulse point. "That was the best night's sleep I've had in a long while." I position myself so I straddle him at the waist, his hardness clearly evident.

"Morning…" I look down at his thick, engorged penis, "glory?"

"Damn no, I could take care of that myself." He takes hold of his cock and pumps it, just the once. "This fucker is rock hard, and that's because I woke up with your sweet ass snuggled up in bed with me." Hooking his hand behind my head, he pulls my face towards him, nearly impaling me on his dick sword. "And the memory of last night." His mouth crashes to mine, his kiss fully charged with electricity that shoots a signal right between my legs. It's hot, it's sexy, and I give him everything I have right back. Sod the morning breath. At this moment, I don't think either of us could care less.

I sit back, a little out of breath, and the aching between my legs is begging me for attention. I lift up onto my knees, positioning myself before taking hold of his cock. We look at each other, not a blink or flicker, as I lower myself slowly, until his cock is fully inside me. Our eyes close, our lip's part, and we both exhale a deep, guttural moan of pleasure.

"Petra," he growls, gripping my hips and pulling me

on to him. I lift, then I drop. Slowly at first, but as my own needs build, so does the momentum. I want to come, and I want him to come too, but I also want more. I push down on him so our bodies are almost fused together and rotate my hips in a circular motion. Holy fuck, it feels so good with his hard cock inside me, filling me. My clit rubs against his pubic bone. His fingers dig into my skin as he moves with me, his moans of pleasure spurring me on. I ride him like I'm on a bucking bronco and no way was I ready to fall yet. His hands move from my hips and cover my breasts. Squeezing them firmly, he tugs at my pebbled nipples. With every stinging pull, I let out a soft moan as it ignites more heat between my legs. I'm so close, so, so close to coming. Then he flips us over so I'm now on my back, and he's in control.

He stops, holding still. I wriggle underneath him, trying to grasp back the sensation that was sending me where I desperately want to be.

"Cade, please."

"Not yet, baby, not until I say you can."

"What, no. Fuck me, Cade, let me come," I growl. Shocking even myself with how harsh I sound. It's like torture.

"You want more of me, baby?" he asks sweetly as he pulls out slowly, then smashes hard back into me. "You want more of my cock?" Slowly out, crashing back in. He leans over me, his mouth up close, his lips skimming over mine as he speaks. "You want me to fuck you hard, baby?"

"Yes, Cade. Yes!" I cry out, my voice deep and almost demonic. My nails digging into his shoulders as I cling onto him. Like hell is he getting away without finishing what I started. "Hard, Cade, hard."

"It's my pleasure."

Hard is not a strong enough word for how he fucks me. It's rough, unrelenting, almost brutal, but it's… simply the most earth shattering, mind-blowing sex I've ever had. Dirty, harsh, and raw, yet I have the most unexplainable feeling of being cared for, cosseted, cherished even. The contradictions, has my head in a spin. Or is it my orgasm that comes with flashing white lights and uncontrollable shakes as I get close to losing consciousness? While the aftershocks take over my body, I barely register the fact that Cade has pulled out of me and is fisting his cock. He ejaculates over my pussy, across my belly, and a few little dots hit just below my boobs. I watch as his fingers run through the sticky cum, spreading it across my skin, like he's marking me, making me his.

I shake the ridiculous notion from my head. It's a fling, a holiday thing. But I'm sure as hell enjoying every frigging minute of it.

We lay side by side on our backs, and allow our heart rates to slowly return to a normal regular beat.

Cade is the first to move, standing at the side of the bed, "Come on, let's get showered off, then I better slip back to my room before Inspector Kat turns up."

My phone pings. I know before I even look at it, it's Kat. It's like she has some sort of voodoo, sixth sense. Every time her name gets mentioned, or I think of her, I get a text or a call, or she turns up out of nowhere.

Cade grabs my purse from where I left it and tosses it

onto the bed beside me.

I get out my phone and open the text message. It's short and sweet and straight to the point. "Breakfast 30 minutes. Shopping."

"I've got to meet Kat in half an hour," I say. He holds out his hand to me and I take it, letting him pull me to my feet. The rush of blood to my head has me wobbling a bit. Catching me, he pulls me to him.

"I'm all sticky," I say, trying to push away.

"Come here," he brings me back to him, holding me so close that our skin becomes almost glued together with the stickiness. "I fucking love it. I like the fact that you smell of me. It's as hot as fuck. I'm not even sure I want you to wash it off."

"Eew, Cade no." I complain, although the thought of having l'eau de Cade on me for the rest of the day is oddly arousing. The smell of him would have me walking around with a girl pecker on 24/7.

"Damn!" he sighs, and I wonder why, but then I feel his hard cock pushing against my stomach. "You should shower first. If I come in there with you, I'm only going to want to fuck you again."

"Oh!" is all I say, but the disappointment in my voice is clearly evident.

"Hey!" he spins me around, facing me towards the bathroom. I feel a wisp of air as he whispers in my ear. "I think that pretty pussy of yours could do with a respite, at least until tonight." He nips my earlobe with his teeth. "Because baby, I might have let you go during the day to placate your buddy Kat, but the nights, you're all mine."

Gently pushing me towards the bathroom, he adds a sharp smack to my bum.

"Ouch!" I grumble, giving him a dirty look over my shoulder as I walk away. But when I turn my head away from him, I can't help the salacious grin that covers my face.

Cade

I'm so tempted to slip into the shower with her, soap up that amazing body of hers, then get her all dirty again. But I don't. I meant what I said. While I want to spend every single minute with her, I know I can't. We have a few days, then she'll be flying back home and I'll go back to Miami.

I pull on my clothes while she's in the shower, deciding that time being limited, I'd be better off getting showered in my room. However, I wait until she's done, as I don't want to go without saying goodbye.

"You're dressed," she says as soon as she sees me. "There's still hot water," she points into the room she came from.

"I know," I reply, walking towards her. "I'll go shower in my room, so you can get ready." Wrapped in a white bathrobe, her olive skin glows from the heat of the shower, she looks up at me with her big brown eyes. I collect a few drops of water that have collected in the hollow of her exposed collar bone with my finger. A waft of berries and vanilla invade my senses, making it impossible to resist putting my arms around her and bring her close, so I can breathe her in. "Come up to my room when you get back."

I don't mean it to sound like a command, but it does. She goes to say something, but I silence her with my determined look. "I don't care what excuse you tell Kat, but you make it happen." I take her mouth, making sure that she knows I mean every single word and that she won't be left disappointed. Letting her go, I take my leave and as I close the door behind me, I instantly feel bereaved. What is this woman doing to me?

When I get to my room, I find Ben slouched on the couch, TV control in hand, as he flicks at great speed from one channel to another.

"Ah, so my brother returns," he says, without turning his attention away from the screen.

I lean across the back of the couch and snatch the control from his hand.

"What the..." he huffs as he stretches out, trying to reclaim the handset. "Guess you got lucky last night," he sniffs and wrinkles his nose. "You stink of sex."

"Stop channel hopping," I bark at him to divert from the line of questioning that Ben is, undoubtedly, wanting to go. "You know it annoys the fuck out of me." I toss the control back to him and he catches it with the skill of a pro baseball player and I make my way to the bathroom.

"So, who was the unlucky victim?" he sniggers. "Don't tell me, let me guess."

"Ben, I need to take a shower." I pull off my shirt as I walk.

"Dark hair, brown eyes, tight little ass that would no doubt look splendid in the flesh."

"Ben," I let out a warning growl.

"And those tits."

"Ben," I say a little louder. My temper rising.

He holds a hand out in front of him, mimicking holding and squeezing one. "Imagine them bouncing in your face when you're fuc..."

"Shut your fucking dirty mouth before I shove the damn TV control up your ass!"

"Woah!" he jumps up, holding both hands in the air in submission. "Calm down, I'm only busting your balls, brother." I glare at him, my fists clenched so hard that the veins in my lower arms pop up. "Shit man, you've got it bad."

"Fucking get out of my face," I rage before stomping off. The bedroom door bounces off the wall with such force that it automatically slams shut behind me.

I throw my balled-up shirt across the room and it hits my pre-determined target, the folded, already worn clothes on the chair. I ferociously unbuckle my belt, push down my trousers and attempt to kick them off my legs, only for them to become caught around my ankles, causing me to temporarily lose my balance. All this does is infuriate me even more. I stand up straight, run my hands through my hair and take a few deep breaths to quench my wrath before walking into the bathroom and into the shower.

I let the water run cool. Hopefully, it will clear my mind, help me make sense of my feelings.

I ask myself...

Why didn't I laugh at Ben's stupid rantings?

Why is the thought of him looking at her in that way, riling me so much?

Why should I care? It's only a few days of no strings attached fucking.

I turn the heat up a little before my balls and dick shrivel up and die from hypothermia. The warmer water begins to run over my head, so I grab the shampoo and start washing. Yet, by the end of my endeavours to get clean, I'm still no wiser as to why this beautiful woman has so easily got under my skin. Or why I have this unequivocal urge to go shopping.

CHAPTER 9

Petra

Tomorrow, Kat and I fly home.

This week has been one hell of a ride. Full of new experiences, laughter, and the best sex that I've ever had.

After spending the days with Kat, I'd wait for the all-clear text from Cade, before sneaking up to his room. We'd have the most incredible sex, order room service, eat, talk, laugh and the have more incredible sex. And every morning I'd wake up next to him.

In general, Cade is the dominant one in all our bedroom antics, but occasionally, he allows me to take the lead for a short while. However, it isn't long before he regains control. I don't complain. I'm happy to be the submissive… in the bedroom.

I also get a glimpse of what I can only describe as his

kinkier side.

It isn't anything major. Holding my wrists tightly above my head, while biting hard on my nipple. Fingering me with more digits than I thought I could take, while slapping my arse cheeks until they are red and tender. It's hot and has me catapulting towards a mega orgasm, every time. It's like he knows exactly how far to go. It has me on edge a little as I sense that, actually, he is holding back. I don't think he'd go too far, or hurt me intentionally, but what scares me is just how far it is that I'm wanting to go. It's a bit of a revelation.

On the other hand, Cade can send me into a total mind-fuck by being so gentle. Touching, caressing, kissing every inch of my body until I'm writhing around, begging for release. For the want of a better word, he makes love to me, so tenderly, leaving me limp, breathless and in a state of euphoria.

However dominant he is when we are having sex, he never is at any other time. Well, not with me anyway. I've overheard a few heated phone calls. Business, I assume, where he is most definitely in charge. He is powerful, demanding, and his level of determination to get the results he wants is staggering. With me, he is funny, kind, and extremely flirtatious.

Amy has mentioned before that he is a bit of a one for the ladies. Had a few in the past that had not wanted to let go of him. One even a little stalkerish. I can see why. He's very charismatic, and I bet he has many a woman tongue tied, starry-eyed and hanging onto his every word. Good job he doesn't practice marital law, otherwise he'd be inundated with offers from newly divorcees.

Bet they'd be only too happy to pay a little extra for his services.

Why the hell am I getting my knickers in a twist at the thought of it? Especially as it's just a short term, holiday type of fling thing. Right?

It's already nine in the evening, and as yet, I haven't heard a word from Cade. A little annoyed at his silence, it being the last chance for us to spend time together, I start haphazardly stuffing my clothes, shoes and items that I've purchased while here, into my suitcase. I try to ignore the lump in my throat when I get a waft of the soaps that Cade bought for me at the market. "Arsehole," I mutter under my breath, blinking rapidly to push back the looming tears.

My phone ping's and I pounce on it. When I see that it's only Kat again, for like the tenth time, asking if I've done my packing. I'm tempted to launch it across the room, until I remember that my contract has another eight months on it yet.

The clothes I intend to travel in are the only things left out, which means I'll only have the shorts and vest top I'm currently wearing and my toiletries to pack in the morning. A few carrier bags are scattered on the floor. My temper getting the better of me, I bring my foot back and kick.

"Ouch!" I scream out when my big toe hits the hard object that's still sitting inside the bag. "Motherfucking hairy ballbags," fires rapidly out of my mouth with a whole load of other not so ladylike profanities. A loud knock at the door has me hopping towards it while nursing my throbbing toe. "For fuck's sake, Kat!" I shout as I open the door. "Get off my back, I'm nearly…" Only to be struck dumb by the sight of Cade. Instantly he notices my hunched over, toe hugging posture.

"What have you done?" he asks, putting his arm around me to support my unstable stance.

"I banged my toe," I reply in a pathetic, whiny voice. I'm so happy to see him that all the built-up, don't really care, he's an arsehole malarkey that had been going through my head, has now gone; 'Poof!' disappeared. I suddenly realise my hand is wet. "Wow!" I stagger when I see red. "Blood."

"Damn, woman," I nearly miss the concern in his voice as my head gets fuzzy. "I can't leave you for a minute." Scooping me up, he carries me to the bed, sitting me on the edge. He takes off at speed into the bathroom, quickly reappearing with a couple of towels and a damp cloth. Kneeling in front of me, he brings my injured foot up to rest on his thigh. I pull it away, worried that he's going to get blood on his trousers. "Let me look," he barks, putting my foot back to where he wants it. I let out a hiss when he lays the damp cloth gently across my toe, as it stings like a bastard. "What did you do?" He looks me in the eye, waiting for an explanation.

"I didn't think you were coming."

"Oh!" he smirks. "Let me guess. You're pissed at me so you decided to kick the… chair?"

"Paper bag actually, but there wasn't meant to be anything in it."

"Ahh!" he lifts he cloth. It's bloody and utterly disgusting. He refolds it until he has a clean area before placing it back. I hiss again. "I'm not sure it's wise telling you this but…" he lets out a deep sigh, "I wasn't going to."

"Fine." My voice cracks a little, but I put my hand to my leg, so it looks like it's from the pain in my foot, not the disappointment in my heart. "But the least you can do is tell my why?"

"Because I didn't want to see you." Removing the cloth, most of the blood now cleaned away, he leans in and inspects it further. "Your nail is pretty smashed and might fall away, but you'll live."

"Well… thank you, but you can leave now. I'm sure I can take it from here." I place my foot on the floor and manoeuvre myself to the side, so I can stand and put some space between us. "Anyhow, I need to finish my packing," I mumble, as I stumble to where my suitcase sits on top of one of those suitcases holding whatsits.

"Petra." I jump at the sound of my name being said right behind me, not realising he's followed so closely. His arms slip around my waist, pulling me back to him. "I didn't want to see you because I can't face saying goodbye."

I shuffle around to face him. Well, it's the best I can do with a poorly toe.

"So, what changed your mind?" I ask with a whisper.

"Because having one more night with you is worth a million sad goodbyes," Cade admits in a deep seductive tone.

Our mouths collide, and our bodies engage as we make the most of our remaining hours together.

Cade

A slither of light hits my face from where the curtain hasn't quite been pulled together. I'm laid on my back with Petra draped over me. Her tits flattened against my chest; her face tucked into my neck. I can hear and feel her every breath as she sleeps in my arms.

Momentarily, I may have considered not coming to her last night, but I couldn't keep away. She's like a drug, a kick, that I know I have to give up. But it won't be easy. Today is when it will end. Petra will go back to her life in Bath, working for Isaac and having girly lunches with Kat and Amy. While as I, will be in the U.S. overseeing my law firm and taking on the big money cases. Maybe it's for the best that we live miles apart. If we kept seeing each other, things would only get… complicated. Women want serious relationships and that's not me. Being tied down, marriage, having damn kids. It's for the best… It sure as hell is for the best.

"Hey," she says sleepily as she stirs in my arms. She snuggles into my neck a little closer, pushes her body into me a little harder before relaxing back and tilting her face up towards me. "Morning."

"Morning, gorgeous." She is gorgeous and so much more. I kiss the tip of her nose and she blinks back at me. Her stunning dark eyes coming alive as a smile lights up her face. God, she's too beautiful for words.

"Better get showered." She suddenly announces and jumps up out of bed. Before I even have time to pull her back, she's walking toward the bathroom.

Her messy bed hair hangs loosely down her back. The curve from her tits to her waist is perfect. The slight sway of her hips when she walks, is so sexy that makes has me salivating. And that ass. It's tight, but not too tight that you don't get a little wobble at the cheeks when she moves. My dick is as hard as fuck from watching her.

"Come back to bed," I bark.

"Sorry, Cowboy," her voice almost singing, coming off weird. "No can do. Time's a wasting." The door closes behind her before I get the chance to say another word.

I wait until I hear the water running before I follow. My plan is to sneak into the shower under a cloak of steam, but when I open the door, I find her stood in front of the vanity, head slumped forward and shoulders dropped. As soon as she hears me, her head snaps up, and she smiles. Even through the mirror's reflection, I can see that it's fake.

"You okay?" I ask and she nods as if afraid to speak. Reaching for her hand, I take hold and guide her with me into the shower cubicle. As I hold her in my arms, I softly stroke her back, and speak loud enough so she can hear me over the noise of the water flow. "Talk to me, Petra."

"I'm fine," she replies. "I've just got the, you know, end of holiday blues. Back to reality and all that."

"So, it's not because you're going to desperately miss me, then?"

"Woah there, Cowboy, be careful, otherwise you're not going to get that gigantic head of yours into your Stetson."

I tilt her chin up to me so she has to meet my gaze. I bring my mouth down to hers so when I speak, my lips brush hers ever so slightly. "Not just a little?" I ask.

"Well, maybe an incy bit," she replies, bringing her pinched up finger and thumb up close to my face to indicate how little.

"Well, I'm going to miss you so fucking much, I…"

When her lips cover mine, I'm lost. All my bravado and utter crap that I was spouting in my head early, purely to convince myself that this was going nowhere, is washed away down the drain.

We kiss, we make love and we hold each other, until the water runs cold and we no longer can avoid the inevitable.

Wrapping a thick white towel around her, I pull her in close, realising that this can't be it. It can't end here.

"I don't want this to end. I know it won't be easy, but we could talk, text, video call. I'll come over as much as I can. I'll pay for your ticket over here. Hell, Isaac and Amy did it." I watch her, as she stares back at me. Her mouth is open and her eyes are wide with surprise. "Damn Petra, say something," the desperation clear in my voice.

"Yes," she whispers. "Yes, yes, yes," she shouts as she jumps up, flinging her arms and legs around me. She clings on to me like a spider monkey, all the while laughing in between our heated kisses. "Now, if I'm not mistaken, there are approximately three hours until I have to leave for the airport."

"Okay, let me order breakfast then I'll help you get your stuff together."

"Fuck that!" she squeals. "I'd much rather spend the time riding my cowboy.

CHAPTER 10

Petra

I'm about ready, but not ready, if you know what I mean. My case is packed, I'm dressed, all I need to do is drag my arse downstairs to meet Kat, where she is currently topping up her caffeine levels. I'm physically ready, but mentally… I so don't want to go home.

After a conversation that bounced back and forth like a Wimbledon tennis final, I've convinced Cade not to come to the airport. Match point to me, when I explained I wanted to say my goodbyes to him in private, and not while being watched by a million and one other commuters.

We kissed, we hugged, all the while holding back the urge to climb him like a tree. So, when my phone pings, telling me it's time, Cade dutifully lets me go with a deep and passionate kiss before collecting my case.

Our journey down in the lift is silent, but looking at each other, our faces portray a thousand 'I'll miss you's'.

We find Kat and Ben stood near the reception desk laughing and joking, acting like it's just another day, not affected by our pending departure in the slightest.

Cade takes my key card from me and walks over to the desk to check me out of my room, leaving me with the annoyingly happy couple.

"You all set?" Kat asks.

"Of course," I reply with fake confidence. "It's been lovely to meet you, Ben." I put my arms around him, giving him a quick, friendly hug. "Hopefully we'll get to see you again soon, maybe spend a little more time together," I say politely.

"You sure will, honey," he laughs. "You've got at least another hour with me. I'm driving you to the airport."

"What?" I gasp and turn to look at Cade, who is walking back towards us. "I thought we agreed?"

"Ben offered to take you both, so..."

"Offered? You demanded, more like," Ben huffs, but with an air of joviality.

"Ben!" Cade runs his hand over his face, then looks at me apologetically. "One minute," he says, holding a finger towards Kat and Ben. He guides me to one side, his hand resting on my hip as he bends to whisper to me. "You won't let me go with you, so Ben is. I need to know that you get there safely." I shake my head at him. "Petra, it's hard enough letting you go as it is. At least grant me this one thing."

"Petra," Kat taps me on the shoulder. "You ready? We

really need to get going."

I look back at Cade and give him a sad smile. "Yes, but you can ride shotgun. I'm going to sit in the back and catch-up on my reading."

We all walk out to the car, Cade and Ben load the suitcases into the boot.

I'm about to climb in when I feel his muscular arm come around my waist, pull me backwards and spin me around to face him. We stand, barely an inch is between us, our gaze securely fixed on each other. Cade steps forward, closing the gap and kisses me so fiercely, everything around us becomes irrelevant. My concern about who might be watching, turns to I don't really give a shit. Ultimately, we become breathless and end our kiss so we can catch our breath. Kat and Ben stand shoulder to shoulder, observing our indiscretion with a knowing smile on their face. Cade finally lets me go when Ben opens the front car door for Kat. Cade's hand rests for a moment in the hollow of my back, while he leans forward to open the back-passenger one.

"Call or text me as soon as you get a chance. Let me know you've got back home safe."

"I will," I reply, as I settle in the back seat. "Thank you."

"What are you thanking me for?" he gives out a soft laugh.

"Just," I also laugh but mine is the nervous kind and I realise that it's not the right time or the right place to discuss my issues, "for making this holiday so memorable."

"Petra darling, believe me when I say, I plan on making more unforgettable moments with you." He puts his cheek to mine and whispers into my ear. "I'm not letting you go."

His words make my heart almost burst with joy and I lean forward and steal another kiss on the lips to seal the deal before relaxing back into my seat. Cade slowly closes the door, a soft smile plays on his lips, while all the time keeping eye contact. Ben gives Cade a brotherly slap on the back and I can just about hear him, as he tells his brother that he needs to get going or we'll miss the flight.

With Cade now stepping back from the car, Ben walks around and gets into the driver's seat. The car engine comes to life and we move away from the curb. I crane my neck to see out the back window, and concentrate on his smile until it no longer can be seen. Then I take in his strong, majestic stature until he's out of sight. With a sigh, I turn back around in my seat and fire up my Kindle. The two in the front are full of chatter. For the fourth or fifth time, I'll be honest I've lost count, I try to read the same page displayed in front of me, but nothing is sinking in. My mind is full of everything that is Cade.

By the time we've said our goodbyes to Ben, finished with check-in and security, the flight has started to board. Thanks to Isaac and his generosity, we board first and get settled into our luxurious First-Class seating. Kat hasn't really said much up to this point, which makes me wonder if I'm not the only one that will miss a new acquaintance in their life.

I should have known better. It was just a matter of time before it began.

"So, you and Cade?"

"What about me and Cade?" I reply in a monotone voice, determined not to give anything away.

"Well, you've pretty much spent every night holed up in his room."

"Eh!" Bloody hell, I should have known nothing would get past her. "How did you find out?"

"I caught the back of you disappearing into the lift one night. It indicated that it was going up, so it was obvious where you were heading," she scoffs.

"I could have been going to see Ben," I countered.

"Doubt it, seeing as Ben was with me. He was as convinced as me, as he's not seen much of Cade either." She raises her eyebrows at me. Her mouth pulled into a tight-lipped, flat smile. "Don't get me wrong, I'm absolutely made up that at last you're back in the saddle," I can't help but snigger, being that I've been calling Cade, Cowboy for the duration of our visit. "But it doesn't take a genius to notice that the way you two were acting, this isn't a fling, is it?"

"He doesn't want it to be."

"Wanting and doing are two different things." My expression must give me away, when she adds. "Bloody hell, Petra, you've fallen for him, haven't you?" she sighs. I don't answer. I close my eyes to hold back the threatening tears and nod. "How the hell are you going to make it work? You're going to be in different parts of the fucking world."

"Believe it or not, there are such things as telephone calls, texts and Skype. He's going to fly over when he can and... I'll go over there." I bark back. A heavy sensation in my gut tells me that a part of me knows exactly where she's coming from and even my defence is weak and sounds unrealistic.

"It's not as easy as that though, is it, love?" her voice becomes softer. "I don't want you to get hurt. I'll be honest, all I can see is this whole thing turning into one big emotional nightmare, and you're the one that's going to come out of it in pieces again."

"I'm different now. Stronger."

"Are you? Really?"

"So, tell me Kat," I turn in my seat, looking her straight in the face. "O wise one. What should I do?"

"Petra, I can't tell you what to do, honey, but in my eyes, you have two options. Finish it now, call an end to it before you get in deeper than you already are. Or, try it, see if you can make it work, but please, go into it with a realistic mind-set, that there is a strong possibility that it's all going to end up smelling of shit." Kat puts her arm around my shoulder and does her best to hug me within the restraints of the seatbelts. "I don't want to open old wounds, and I know that you hate to talk about your last breakup, but it near on killed me to watch you go through it. I don't want to do it again, but whatever you decide, I'll be right here by your side."

The tears are unstoppable, as they spill down my cheeks and she pats my knee with her free hand to comfort me, like she is the mother and I'm the grazed kneed kid.

"I… I… gues… sss, I've got some thinking to do," I stutter between sobs. "Is the bar opening yet?"

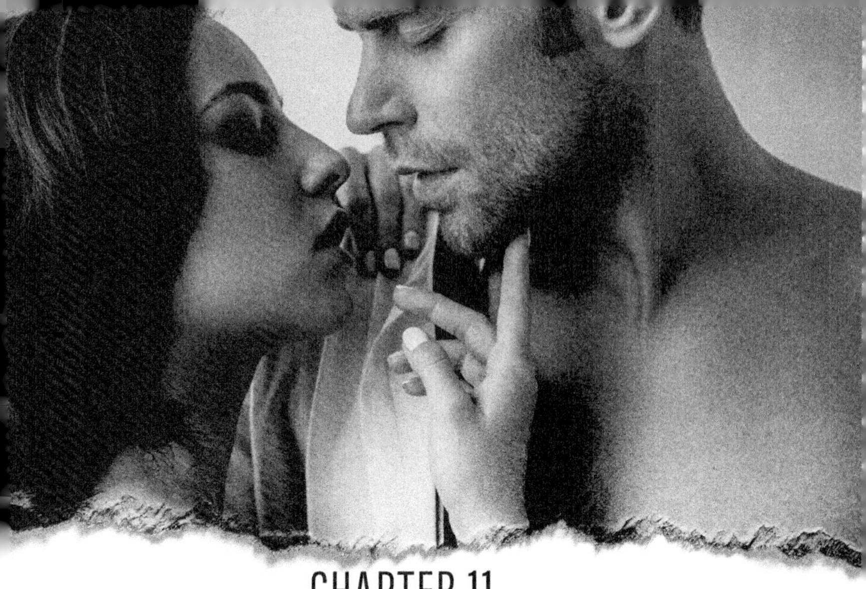

CHAPTER 11

Petra

First day back at work and the jet lag is kicking my arse.

Yesterday, on our return, as Kat and I have apartments in the same building, we said our goodbyes in the lift, before I stepped out at my floor. When I walked into my place, I was hit with the familiar smell of my vanilla plug-in air-freshener, and a slight chill in the air from the rooms being unoccupied for over a week. For the first time in a long time, it didn't feel that good to be home.

So, I was glad that I was straight back to work, simply to keep my mind occupied and off the subject of Cade.

I had texted him to say that I was home safe, but shattered and needed to get some sleep, as I was due back to work the next day. His reply was short and curt. However, he said that he would video call tonight at 7.30 UK time.

I've made my decision. At least I think I have. The arguments for and against that are going on in my head make it difficult to think rationally. Has Cade already decided that this is more trouble than it's worth?

I'm more trouble than its worth?

But if that's the case, wouldn't he have sent a text? No, I don't think Cade would do that, he'd look someone in the face if he had something to tell them.

Oh, video call.

It doesn't matter, anyway. I'm calling it off. Kat's right. Better to get out now before I'm in too deep. I hope I get lucky, and he makes it easy for me by being the one who does the dumping.

At 7.15 I'm sat on my sofa, iPhone in hand, waiting for the call. I've practiced my little speech for what seems like a zillion times, while showering and dressing in some comfy lounge clothes. I don't want to look like shit, but I don't want to look like I've made too much of an effort, either. My reasons for putting a stop to this 'relationship' sounds pathetic, the more I repeat it, stumbling over my words every time. It doesn't sound very believable either.

I jump when my phone comes to life, vibrating and playing one of the God-awful preloaded tunes that has the appropriate sound of doom.

I quickly smooth down my hair, paint on a fake smile, and answer. The screen lights up and the image I see has me gasping and laughing at the same time.

Cade dressed in nothing but a Stetson hat perched on his head, is not what I expected to see. The camera is strategically placed so I can see the expanse of his upper toned body and his glorious V, but not the goods down below. He is completely naked unless his pants are pushed down and resting around his ankles.

"Well, howdy there, little darling." His impression of a cowboy is more like Woody from Toy Story than Kevin Costner.

"Are you in your office?" I giggle, taking in the large window in the background that depicts the skyline of a multitude of tall office buildings.

"Don't worry, most of the staff are out or having lunch in the canteen. The door's locked and no one can see me."

"What about the window cleaner?" I point to somewhere behind him with the best possible serious face I can come up with.

He twists around so fast that his chair tips backwards, almost going over. If it wasn't for the speed of Cade rectifying it, I'm sure I would have got a fabulous look at his penis.

"Just kidding," I laugh.

"Bad girl," he scowls, wagging a finger at me. "For that I think I might have to make you do a forfeit."

"Oh really? And what exactly do you suggest my penance should be?" I reply. I'm nervous and excited all at the same time as to where this is going, but I know when it comes to Cade, my resilience is wafer thin.

"However, much as I enjoy seeing your beautiful face, I want to see more."

Wow, those few words in that deep American accent, from those slightly pouty lips, have my heart racing and thighs clenching. Oh, that mouth. That mouth that spent so much time on various parts of my body.

Jesus, I think I'm going straight to hell. My thoughts are dirty and sinful.

I'm lost and I don't think I want redemption.

"Put the camera further away so I can see all of you."

"Erm! I don't know…"

"Do as I ask, Petra." His tone is firm, not harsh, but it's enough to have me up on my feet to grab a couple of books from my bookcase so I can prop my phone up on the coffee table in front of me.

"Damn!" he curses out. "You look so fucking hot."

"Cade," I laugh nervously, "I'm in shorts and a vest."

"Yeah, but the way your nipples are pushing against the fabric is fucking sexy. Are you as turned on as me?"

"What, no, erm…" I automatically cross my arms over my chest. "It's a little draughty in here, that's all."

"Really?" he raises an eyebrow. "Don't cover yourself. I missed looking at you. Lean forward a little so I can see more. In fact, forget that, take your shirt off."

"I… I." God, I'm so aroused I'm already wet. This is not how I expected this to go. I was expecting this to be awkward for a different reason. Come to think of it, it's not awkward, just different.

"Let me see you." I can tell that he's already becoming aroused by his deep, gravelly voice. I don't hesitate any further. I whip my top off over my head and expose my breasts. My nipples are already standing to attention, but hell if they don't stand out further, as if trying to get nearer to Cade.

"Holy shit, baby, its torture not being able to touch you, but looking at you, is making me so fucking horny."

"Me too," I admit. I lay the palms of my hands over my nipples, but all it does is send a shot of heat straight between my legs. I bite on my bottom lip to try to stifle the moan that threatens to escape me. With Cade watching me closely, I'm sure that I haven't fooled him.

"Are you wet, Petra?" he growls.

"Mmm," is all I manage.

"Open your legs for me and show me."

I slide my legs apart and I'm sure that the evidence of my arousal can be clearly seen on the fabric at the apex of my legs. The temptation to put my hand there is more than I can bear and when my fingers slide across the wet patch, the guttural moan that comes from Cade immediately captures my attention.

His eyes are so hooded that they look almost closed, mouth partially open as he pants in and out, a growl that reminds me of a prowling animal. His hands grip the arms of the chair, his fingers digging into the padding of the upholstery. At the bottom of the screen, you can see the head of his hard cock as it bobs up and down in shot, as if it's playing a dirty game of hide and seek. Now you see me. Now you don't.

The echo of a loud knocking sound has us both snapping out of our erotic screen playing and a mumbled voice shouting Cade's name.

"I'm busy. Come back in twenty minutes!" He shouts out. "I don't care, it can wait."

"Cade," I whisper at the screen, worried that I might

give the game away. "Maybe you should go."

"Damn it," he slams his hand on the armrest before standing. His still hard cock, with its glistening tip, fills the whole screen until he pulls up his trousers. I get an encore while he tries to manoeuvre his man meat in his pants, so he doesn't catch it with the zip. "I'm sorry. Can I call you later?" The screen jiggles about a bit until he brings it nearer to himself, so all I now see is his perfect face.

"I might be in bed."

"Hell, don't tease me. I'm struggling to get the image of you out of my head as it is." He wipes the tiny beads of perspiration from his forehead with the back of his hand. "Let me call. I'll try not to make it too late."

"I'll try, but if I don't answer, it's because the jetlag has wiped me out, okay?"

"Good. I better go before they bang down the door." Silence falls, and we both stare at the screens in front of us. If only I could reach out and touch.

"Petra."

"Yes?" silence. I watch as he runs his fingers through his dishevelled hair, then slides his hand down his face.

"I… I'll call later."

"Okay." Silence hits again. Neither of us makes the move to end the link.

"In case we don't speak later. Goodnight, Petra."

"Goodnight, Cade."

When his face disappears from the screen and he's replaced with an image of my favourite book cover model, it's clear to me that however difficult this may be and how big the risk is of it all coming crashing down on me like a big nasty pile of shit, I can't walk away from this chance of having something special and exciting with this most captivating man.

CHAPTER 12

Petra

The month since we got back from Florida has seemed to drag so slowly, it makes a turtle look like its turbo charged. I throw myself into work, trying to keep busy and do my utmost to be the ultimate professional. But as soon as my phone pings, and I see that it's Cade, I sneak off to the bathroom so I can spend some private time with him. Well, his text messages anyway.

I know it's crazy, but I also know that I have the stupidest of smiles slapped on my face, which would have the rest of the staff asking questions that, at the moment, I'm not prepared to answer. It might jinx it.

We've not video called again, yet. But every other day he calls me late at night. He says he loves to hear my sexy as fuck sleepy voice. I can relate. Maybe not sleepy, but his voice has me tingling from head to foot. If he did advert voice overs, he'd have the women swooning and clearing the shelves in the nearest store of whatever he was pitching. If it was vibrators and condoms, there'd be a lot of thrilled, satisfied customers.

When the phone wakes me suddenly, I quickly check my alarm clock and see that it's just gone midnight. My heart pounds when I see Cade's name light up on the screen of my phone. I only spoke to him last night. A giant knot of worry sits heavy in my stomach as I answer the call.

"Hello."

"Hey baby, you're awake?"

"Well, I am now." I don't mean to be snarky, but this feeling of dread is making me angsty. "Where are you?"

"Miami. I know it's late… I… I shouldn't have rung."

"Cade, it's fine. What's up?"

"I needed to hear your voice."

"Has something happened?" I ask, pushing myself up to a sitting position. "Is everything okay? Ben, Isaac, Amy?"

"Everyone's fine. I had a terrible day and I… God, I wish you were here with me."

"How bad is bad?"

"The case I've been working on, some little guy against a big conglomerate. It should have been a done deal, but the company's hot shot lawyer had them walking away scot-free on a technicality." He mumbles a few choice words under his breath. "I should have picked up on it, but I missed it."

"Isn't that the nature of the game, that you can't possibly win them all?"

"I know. I can't go into too much detail, but it's pretty much ruined this guy's life, when it's blatantly obvious that the company was at fault. He has a young family and another kid on the way, now he's been left with a whole load of debt, unable to work, which means he's going to lose his home."

"That is pretty shitty," I sympathise. "Isn't there anything you can do to help?"

"I've wavered my fees, but that's about as much as I can do," he sighs. "God, he must be worried sick about providing for his family. I'm glad I don't have that sort of responsibility."

"I guess." I'm not sure what I can say to ease his stress over all this. I'm clueless about this type of legal stuff.

"I'm sorry, I shouldn't be burdening you with all my crap."

"Cade, I'm not sure what I can say or do to make this any better, but if you need to vent, I'm always here to listen."

"Baby," he laughs softly. "You make everything seem better."

"In that case, I'm glad to be of service."

"Anyway. How's things with you?" he asks changing the subject.

"Okay, nothing new to tell, really. I'm having lunch next week with Amy. She's going to be back here, but Isaac has to stay in New York for an extra week. I think she wants to drag me around a few baby shops. I'd rather go around a few bars, but I guess that's out of the question for a while."

"Yeah, can you believe that? Isaac knocked her up already."

"He's happy about it though, isn't he?"

"Oh yeah. Look at how he is with Mikey. He adores the kid."

"They do make a cute couple," I agree on a sigh.

"Talking about Isaac, he's asked me to come over there next month, so…"

"Really?" Suddenly. I'm super awake. The excitement builds, but I try not to let it get to boiling point. "You're coming here?"

"I'd have been there sooner, if it hadn't been for this damn case. I have a few things I need to get done, but then I'll be flying over for a week. Looks like Isaac will have me tied up most of the time, but the evenings are for you."

"When do you get here?" I'm gripping the phone hard, trying to keep myself grounded.

"I've not got the confirmed date yet, but I'll message you as soon as I do. Make sure you're free, because I'm planning on spending as much time with you as possible."

"Cade."

"Yes?"

"I can't wait to be with you." My breathing is uneven and my voice deep and sultry.

"Oh, baby. Say that again."

CHAPTER 13

Cade

Every day for the last month has seemed to drag, but at last I'm walking up the tunnel off the BA206 flight at Heathrow Airport. It's 7.45 am, which makes me over an hour later than scheduled, and I'm hoping that Isaac checked the departure of my flight before setting off to collect me. If not, he's going to be pissed.

I've not flown into this airport for a long time, but with Isaac's decidedly descriptive directions, I collect my checked-in bag and find my way to our meeting point with ease.

Isaac is standing with his back to me, talking on his phone and oblivious to my arrival. I sneak up behind him. It becomes apparent that he's talking to Amy because of the sweet nothings he's saying. I get up close, making sure I don't touch him, but near enough to lean in nearer to the handset.

"Oooh! Isaac, sugar, who are you talking to?" I say in my best high pitched, lady impression. As Isaac spins around, it's clear I'm not fooling anyone as I hear Amy's laugh and the words "Hi Cade," filter across the airwaves.

"Hi sister-in-law," I holler back, having to shout because Isaac has already bumped me away with his elbow.

"So, the answer to your question is yes, he has arrived, finally." Isaac continues his conversation with Amy, but not missing the chance to throw me a stern look. "Okay, I'll let you know when we get back to the office... Yes baby, I do too." Isaac finishes the call and stands firm footed in front of me.

"You're so pussy whipped, brother," I say, shaking my head in disgust.

"You're such a jackass, brother." He barks back before we pull each other into a man hug, giving each other a slap or two on the back. "I've missed you, you asshole."

"The feelings mutual." The closeness we share, no one would believe that we weren't true blood.

"The car's out this way in the parking lot." He indicates to the exit. We start to walk in that direction. "What's with the suitcase, are you planning on stopping more than a couple of days?"

"Seven days, but don't worry brother, I won't be imposing on you and Amy, as the last thing I need to listen to, is the sound of you two fucking every chance you can get."

"Do I sense a touch of jealousy?" Isaac sniggers. "Not

been getting enough, big boy?"

"I do more than alright douche-bag."

"You know Amy won't hear of you stopping in a hotel when we have plenty of room for you to stay with us. I'll put you as far away from our room as possible. She doesn't mind being gagged either, so you won't hear a thing."

"What the fuck, Isaac. I really don't need to hear that shit." We stop at the side of a black Audi Q8 and Isaac pops the trunk. I place my suitcase in the back and walk towards the passenger side. Isaac follows me and then I notice the steering wheel, I change direction and walk around to the other side. Isaac shakes his head and laughs at my error. I show him my middle finger across the roof of the car before getting in.

"Anyway, I'm not staying at a hotel. If all goes well, I'll be staying with someone." I offer as we pull away from the airport perimeter.

"Who?"

"Just a friend."

"You? Friends?" Isaac gives out a loud chuckle. "Didn't realise you had any."

"Fuck you, asshole." I punch him in his bicep and by the feel of it, he's still hitting the gym regularly. "Just drive and less of the verbal crap."

We chat idly and get to the Bath office in record time. Mainly due to Isaac being unable to resist showing off some of his driving skills that he picked up in his younger years. Skills that were useful back in the day, when he was stealing cars to make enough money to get a discount motel and put food in his stomach.

He's not proud of what he did back then, but he was homeless, and what little cash he had, when he ran away from home, went quickly. It seemed to be the only option at the time, his only chance of survival.

When you see him now, what he's achieved, you can't help but admire him for the man he has become. He insists it was all thanks to my dad, for taking in him, bringing him into our family and the faith he had in him. Truth is, Isaac has worked his butt off to get to where he is today. His pure determination to change his world. From dirty back alley and breaking the law, to a law-abiding citizen, earning his own money, thriving businesses and keeping people in jobs. My admiration for him is vast. My respect for him huge. His actions are the reason why I worked tirelessly to get my law degree and, in turn, excel in everything that I do. He inspires me. But I'll be damned if I'll ever tell him.

***

Two hours later, I can feel the fatigue consuming my whole body, and I can barely keep my eyes open.

"Come on Cade, you're beat," Isaac says, getting up from his seat and walking around to the opposite side of the desk where I sit. "Why don't you go get some sleep and we can talk again tomorrow."

"Hell," I push myself up to a standing position. "Not until you show me around. I've always wondered what was so special about this place that made you want to invest."

"To get the girl," he smiles as he rubs the back of his

neck. I look at him, waiting for more of an explanation. "Long story," he laughs. "Come on, let me give you a guided tour."

I'm really not that interested, but by the sounds of it, Isaac is looking for me to get involved with the companies he owns. I play along, but the only reason I want to look around is that I'll get to see Petra. Fuck waiting until tonight. I'm desperate to have something, albeit a quick glance of those deep brown eyes, sun kissed olive skin and pout of her lush mouth.

We go from office to office, as he introduces me to colleague after colleague, not one of the nameplates on the doors showing the one that I'm looking for. I'm about to lose my shit when I see it. 'Personnel/Payroll Department'. She's just beyond this door. I stop next to the door, but Isaac keeps on walking.

"Hey buddy, you missed one!" I almost shout without thinking.

"No point, there's no one in there today."

"Yeah, don't tell me you have them on one of those pointless team-building exercises," I laugh lightly.

"Unfortunately, no," he sighs. "Judy has left us. Caroline is on vacation. I told the trainee to go home as she has no one to supervise her because Petra… you know Petra, she was at the wedding, she's had to take emergency leave."

"Is she okay?" My gut feels like it's been hit with a ten-pound hammer.

"I don't know the full story, but Kat… you know Kat, she was at the wedding too. She said that Petra's mother is sick, and she had to fly back to Slovakia."

"Oh, poor girl." I mumble, trying not to show my mixed-up feelings of concern and disappointment.

"Yeah, I'm sure Amy will know more. Look, it's nearly 4pm, why don't we call it a day. Come back to the house, have a couple of beers, dinner and then I'll get you a cab to drop you at your friends later?"

"Sounds good to me," I plaster a fake smile on my face. "In fact, if the offer to stay with you is still open, then I'd like to take you up on that, for tonight."

"Fucking A," Isaac smacks me hard on the back. "Brother, you're more than welcome. I miss your sorry ass. It's good to have you here."

***

Isaac and Amy are the most gracious of hosts, and I can't help laughing along with them. Their happiness is as contagious as a dose of influenza. It helps me handle the fact that after many attempts to contact Petra; I keep coming up blank. It's not until late the next day that I finally get a response. It's only a text, but it's better than nothing.

Petra: Sorry. Family emergency. Talk soon.

I text her back asking if it's convenient to call her, because to be honest, however pissed I am that she's taken so long to respond, I need to know what's going on. I want to support her anyway I can. According to Amy, who doesn't have that much more information than Isaac, Petra's mum is not good and being the only child, she's having to handle this on her own. The response is almost immediate.

Petra: Not now. I'll call you soon.

CHAPTER 14

Cade

It's the night before I fly back to Miami, and I still haven't spoken to Petra. I've stayed the whole time with Isaac and Amy, and I'm sure by now they'll be glad to see the back of me when I board the early flight in the morning.

Amy has been a godsend, with her constant chatter and positivity. It's distracted me from thoughts of Petra that infiltrate my mind. Well, sometimes.

I send another text, telling her I'm going to call and that she better pickup. It's a little harsh, but I don't really care anymore. I can't stand the not knowing. I need to know what the fuck is going on. She replies…

Petra. Okay.

I read the one-word message several times while I calm myself, then hit the call button.

"Hello." There's an unusual hardness to her normally soft voice.

"Hi," is all I say although a mountain of questions goes through my head.

"Cade, I'm sorry but I can't do this."

"Do what, Petra?"

"I can't... It was fun, it's over. I don't have time for you in my life anymore."

"You can't be serious? You don't have time for a phone call, a text message?"

"Exactly. It's a joke Cade, that's not and never will be a relationship." I'm sure I hear a crack in her voice. "The only thing that's important in my life is here, here in Bratislava, so I'll be staying over here."

I'm a lawyer. I should be able to argue my side, put up a good fight, but I can't seem to break down the barriers that are holding me back.

"Take care, Cade," she chokes out when I don't respond. I know that she's crying.

"Petra..." I breathe, but the call has already ended. I immediately try to call her back, but all I get is an irritating computerised voice, telling me my call can't be taken right now. I throw my phone across the room, and it smashes to the floor.

The words she spoke go around in my head.

'I don't have time for you in my life anymore'

'It's a joke,'

'It's over,'

It's over.

CHAPTER 15

Sam's 1st birthday party
Isaac and Amy's Bath Home.

Cade

I can't believe she's here.

I watch her from the corner of my eye, stood at the other side of the room with Kat, talking to Ben. Awesome. Now Nessa has walked up to join them. It pisses me off that I'm excluded. Even with the hint of a dark shadow under her eyes, Petra is fucking stunning. Looking at her makes all the past year and God knows how many months seem to disintegrate. The hurt is still as poignant as the day she told me it was over.

I know I should talk to her, at least be civil, but I don't. I end up sitting in the damn chair, sulking like an adolescent schoolboy.

"Hey, big man," Amy says as she puts a gentle hand on my shoulder. "You okay? You seem a little distracted."

"Yeah, yeah, I'm good," I can't help glancing in Petra's direction, but I quickly return my attention to Amy, hoping she didn't notice. "Just a bit of jet lag. How are you, Amy? Is my brother looking after you?"

"Your brother treats me like a China doll and you know it," she laughs. "I think it's time for the birthday cake. I'll go get it from the kitchen." And she scoots off again.

I get up out of my seat and walk towards the group, tapping Ben on the shoulder, my excuse to get closer to Petra.

"Excuse me," Petra blurts. "I… I need to have a word with Amy." Blatantly, she avoids eye contact with me and walks off towards the kitchen.

"What have you done?" Ben, the ever-tactful moron, blurts out.

"I have done nothing," I snap back.

"Well, you must have done something. Woah! She was like… out of here."

"I'll go check on her." Kat disappears into the kitchen, but it's not long before they both come back out, their heads together as they chatter. Isaac walks past them and enters the kitchen.

"Damn, that kitchen is like grand central station with people coming and going," Ben chortles.

Petra turns her back to us and carries on talking to Kat. I'm not sure if it's my paranoia, but the way Kat keeps glancing over, I'm sure that it's me that's the hot topic of conversation.

"You can't avoid him forever, Petra." Kat blurts out.

"Who said I can't," I reply, my head bowed, looking up at her through my lashes.

"You know that this has gone on for far too long. That wall that you build up around yourself, doesn't protect you Petra, it keeps out everyone who tries to get close to you."

"I don't need anyone else in my life. I have you and mum and…"

"I know I was sceptical at first but, I really thought that Cade was good for you. I actually thought that he'd managed to get you to realise that you can't let people in your past, influence your future." The lights dip into almost darkness, making it easier for me to hide my burning anger from the others in the room.

"Don't start raking up my past, Kat," I growl back at her through gritted teeth. "If you ever think I'm going to risk that happening again, months of therapy, have my world turned upside down, because of a man. You're mistaken."

"But what about…" A loud crash gets all our attention and one by one we rush to the kitchen only to find Amy on the floor along with a messed-up birthday cake. Gooey chocolate, strawberries with squished yellow lettering that you could only make out the words 'Hap B am.'

Isaac immediately drops to his knees beside her, stroking her hair, his soft voice coaching her back to him. "Amy, Amy, wake up for me, baby!" Her eyes flutter as she slowly becomes lucid.

"What happened?" she asks, looking around at the many concerned faces that are watching her. Suddenly, she bursts into tears. "Oh shit, Isaac, I think I'm pregnant!"

A mix of laughter, mutterings of congratulations and I think someone even clapped, before we slowly filter out of the room, giving Isaac and Amy some privacy.

Grabbing my purse from the side unit where I'd left it earlier, I make my way to the downstairs toilet, only to find that it's already occupied. Knowing the layout of the house and that Amy won't mind, I nip up the stairs so I can use the house bathroom. After doing what us girls need to do, including checking for face shine and topping up the lippy, I leave the bathroom. On stepping out into the hallway, I find Cade leant against the wall, directly opposite.

"Petra."

"Sorry to have kept you waiting, the bathroom's free now." I say as I continue to walk away.

"Wait." He catches my upper arm, stopping me in my tracks. I turn to face him, but I can't quite meet his eyes. "How are you?"

"I'm fine, thank you."

"And your mother?"

"Things are much better than they were," I reply a little evasively, as I don't want to get into some full-on conversation. However, I feel a bit of a shit and having been brought up with manners, I can't help but ask. "How are you?"

"Missing you." His voice is barely audible, but I know exactly what he said.

"Cade," I drop my head and watch my fidgeting feet.

"Let's not go there."

"Go where?" his voice has become agitated and louder. "Back to where you tell me I'm not worth it, that I'm a joke. Is that what it was to you, Petra? Just a bit of fun?"

"That's not what I said and you know it. I couldn't… didn't want to be with you anymore."

He pushes me back against the wall and places his body up close to mine. For all intents and purposes, I'm caged in. This does nothing but cause a rush of excitement to every part of me. When his hand moves to my rib cage, above my waist and dangerously close to the round of my left breast, my arousal begins to burn. He supports himself with his other hand pressed against the wall, right next to my head, he leans into me. I keep my head low, knowing that if I look at his face, his eyes, his lips, all my ability to resist him will shatter.

"Couldn't or didn't?" his mouth is so close to mine that his breath is cold against my glossy lips. Yet still I refuse to meet his gaze. "I think you need to clarify, as they are two very different things, Petra. Very different things."

"What's the matter Cade, can't your ego accept I don't want you. That for once you were the one being dumped?" I smirk at him. My breath hitches when his thumb strokes across the mound of my breast, flicking over my already prominent nipple. My traitorous body lets out a disgruntled sigh when he takes his hand away, it's already internally screaming for more. Placing his index finger under my chin, he tilts my face to his until I have no option but to look him in the eye.

"You might say that you don't want me, but your body

is giving me all the right signals." His lips hover over mine as he whispers, "Did you miss me, baby?"

I push up on my tiptoes and push my lips to his. Instantly, his tongue slips into my mouth and I caress it with my own. A deep, guttural moan comes from deep within his throat. His hands cup my face as he deepens the kiss.

It feels so good, so deliciously right, but then the voice of reason in my head speaks up and verbally kicks my arse. This can't happen.

With all the strength I have, I push him away with both hands, creating a small amount of space between us.

"No," I pant. "I'm sorry, this is a mistake." I sidestep, turn on my heels and move fast, almost stumbling as I flee down the steps like a drunken Cinderella at a fucked-up ball. I hear him call my name, a curse and a loud bang, but I don't turn back. I walk straight out of the house, get straight in my car, and drive away.

It's not until I'm parked outside my apartment that I let myself go. I can barely see what I'm texting when I send a message to Kat. I don't go into details. I tell her to pass on my apologies. To tell them I'm unwell, and that I've left and gone home. The text I get back is short and not so sweet. Just the one word.

Liar!

And I know that tomorrow, I'll have some explaining to do.

CHAPTER 16

Cade

It's been three months since Petra ran, and I still get pissed when I think about it. I could have run after her, but what's the point. I got the next flight back to Miami and threw myself back into my work. When I wasn't concentrating on my current case, my mind would inevitably slip back to her. It was driving me crazy, so I spent most of my spare time pushing myself to the max at the gym. It's not one of those high-class places you pay $200-$300 dollars just for the joining fee. It's a seedy backstreet place that's like something out of Rocky but with a lot of weights and a few treadmills. Axe, Isaac's old friend, recommended it. Apparently, the old guy who owns it had been like a dad to him in his younger days. Even shown him how to box. After working out, if anyone's about, I offer myself up for a sparring session. I'm shit at it, and even with the headgear, many a time I end up with a bruise or two. It sure as hell doesn't look good when I'm due in court the next day. I've also got into a routine when leaving the gym, of going straight to the bar close by. One drink, I tell myself. But many a time I end up pushing the boundaries, ending up drunk, barely able to call a cab.

The liquor doesn't stop me thinking about her, doesn't stop her beautiful face coming to me in my dreams. Hot illicit sex scenes plaguing me in my alcohol induced sleep. But at least the next day, I don't remember them. Not clearly, anyway.

I've picked up a few random women, had sex around the back of a few of the bars. Every fucking time that I do manage to get my release, it's with the image of Petra firmly imprinted in mind. It's cheap and nasty and it makes me feel like shit. Yet I still go and do it again.

I know I'm behaving like a jackass. Even Ben's been on my case, telling me to get my shit together. And I tell myself every day that today is going to be different, that I'm going to go home, watch a game, have a beer and chill. Because when it comes down to it, I don't do relationships; I don't want commitment. I'm perfectly fine on my own. That's how it has been and that's how it's going to stay. I don't need anyone invading my world. But when the clock hit's 19:00 hours, I slip straight into the same routine and end up in the same old sorry state.

My head pounds with every shrill that my phone makes, waking me. The sun hits my face and I curse myself for being so drunk last night that I didn't even draw the blinds. Even the light of my phone is painfully bright. Screwing my eyes up, I try to make out who is calling me at such a God early hour. It's Isaac.

I've been avoiding him like the plaque, giving him one excuse after another as to why I can't make it over to Bath. Caught on the hop, I quickly try to think of a plausible excuse while hitting the answer button.

"What?" I bark down the phone, my voice as gravely as shit from the all the liquor.

"Woah! You got out of the wrong side of the bed this morning?" Isaac's deep and jovial voice makes my head pound even more. "Or was it simply the wrong bed in the first place?"

"If you must know I'm still in bed, do you know what the fucking time is?"

"Time to get your ass up, pack a bag, so you can head to the airport."

"What the hell are you talking about, I rescheduled for next week."

"And I rescheduled it back, so you better get your shit together."

"I've got plenty of time."

"Cade, are you shitting me? You don't even know what time it is, do you?" My answer to him is a mumbled groan, as I push my head into the pillow to try to cushion the aching. "It's 19.22 hours over here, so that means it's around 14.22 over there. Your flight is at 17.10 so you better move it."

"What the fuck Isaac, cancel the damn thing. I won't make it in time, anyway." I push myself up and move to sit on the edge of the bed.

"The hell you won't," he barks down the phone. "You

should have been here weeks ago, so don't you fucking let me down again."

"You're quite capable of taking care of business without me, Isaac. It's not like you've not done this shit before."

"Not this time. This time, it's way above my head, so I need you here, brother. Otherwise, my business is in jeopardy." There's an uneasy tone in Isaac's voice that I've not heard in a long while. I run my hand down my face, roll my head, albeit slowly, flex my shoulders before getting up, a little unsteadily to my feet.

"Send me the flight details and e-ticket."

"Already done. I'll be tied up at the office all day, so Amy will be there to pick you up."

"I can grab a car, drive myself." Don't get me wrong, I like Amy a lot. But I'm not in the mood for nearly two hours of girly chat. That will undoubtable turn to subjects that I'm not willing to or want to discuss.

"Wouldn't hear of it. Besides, it will be good for you both to spend some more time together, get to know each other a little better. See you in the morning." In typical Isaac style, the phone goes dead before I even get a chance to plead my case.

Two hours later, I hit the airport running. The traffic in Miami is manic, so by the time I get there, it's touch and go whether I make it to the check-in just in time. Isaac has me booked first class, so with a smile and a brief flirtation, I talk my way on to the flight. Security is a pain, but I understand that it's necessary, it's a shame that in the world we live in today, it's come to this. As luck would have it, I at least have decent socks on when I had to remove my shoes, and miraculously, a matching pair.

With the help of a couple of Advil, I sleep through most of the flight. I kind of hope that it might help alleviate the blood-shot eyes and the shadows that have taken up residence below them. The flight is on time and my ride's waiting. Amy doesn't see me at first, so I take this rare chance to appraise her. Her stance is a little awkward. To be honest, it looked like her thoughts are somewhere else, probably on one of the kids, or Isaac. She seems oblivious to most of what is going on around here. If you wrote down on paper her general description, you would come up with nothing special. But she is so damn lovely in face, body, and soul, that I know exactly why Isaac has fallen truly, madly and deeply in love with her. I know I yank his chain sometimes, but he's certainly got himself a real gem. If truth be known, I don't just admire and respect Isaac. I'm a little jealous of him too. It's clear that Amy adores Isaac, and he radiates because of it. Something that I doubt I'll ever get to experience.

Amy catches sight of me and gives me an excited wave.

"Cade, you're here. Oh, my God, you look like shit."

"Nice to see you too," I tut, before placing a soft kiss on her cheek. A soft blush covers her face, another endearing quality to add to her list. "I've heard of evil step-mothers," I hold my hands up in submission before she hits, "of which unquestionably you are not." She drops her partially raised hand. "But is there such a thing as evil sisters-in-law?" Slap! I don't know when to stop sometimes. Seems like Ben's not the only one that talks too much.

"You've got to be kidding me?" I laugh in amazement when Amy stops beside Isaac's prized possession, his Aston Martin Vanquish Ultimate Grand Tourer. The shine on the deep red paintwork is like a mirror. The windows, trim and even the wheels are spotless, as if it's been driven off the lot. "You've definitely got him wrapped around your little finger, if he's letting you drive this."

"Don't I just," she replies smugly as she pops the trunk. When I go to lift my suitcase in, I can see empty tote bags, a pair of lady's pumps and a rather tatty umbrella, leaving me stood with my mouth open. "You go for groceries in this?" I ask, when I get past my initial shock.

"Only if I haven't got Sam with me, it's not really made for baby seats," she replies nonchalantly, as she closes the trunk and walks around to get into the driver's side. Suddenly, she stops and turns to me. "Do you want to drive?" She spins the key chain on her finger.

"Are you shitting me?"

"Did you drink on the plane?"

"Not a drop, I just slept."

"Then why not? If you want to that is? Don't you have a sporty car at home, anyway?"

"Sure, I have a Corvette Stingray, but this?" I walk towards her and take the keys from her hand, a mischievous smile across my face. "But this is Isaac's car. You do know he'll go crazy?"

"Well, I won't tell him if you don't," she laughs, skipping around to the passenger side.

My Corvette is pretty neat, but the interior of this car is pure class. The cream leather with quilted trim is soft like butter. The centre console and dash are a sleek, shiny black with a touch of silver. Not in your face opulence. Clean, sharp and super stylish. Once I manage to get my 5'11" frame into the space set for Amy's 5' nothing, I adjust the seat to suit me. It's when I go to start the car that I realise its shift drive and although I've driven shift before, I know this ride is going to be like a bucking bronco, until I get comfortable with it.

By the time we hit the M4, I've got the hang of it and Amy's controlled her fits of giggles at my inexperience with gears.

"Thank God for that," she sighs, rubbing the slight roundness of her stomach. "This little mite must have thought it was on a trampoline."

"Jesus, are you okay?"

"Of course, I'm okay," she laughs. "I'm from Yorkshire don't forget, and I've had rougher rides." I don't quite understand what she means until I catch sight of the wink and the flush of her skin.

"You are extremely beautiful, Mrs Rice, especially when you blush. Underneath, I think you are a contradiction to your innocent outer exterior. One, I'm sure, of which my brother takes great delight in."

"Cade! Are you flirting with me?"

"That, my sweet sister-in-law I can categorically say, I am not." I fake gasp. "Although I do think you lost out when you picked the inferior brother and not the superior one."

"Ben wasn't interested, so I went for the next desirable

option." She quirks back, with a highly impressive straight face.

"Shit!" I shake my head at her. "You're good."

"So, brother-in-law. Let's cut the crap. Tell me, what's going on between you and Petra?"

"Petra?" The mention of her takes me by surprise. "Why would you think there was something going on? I hardly know the woman."

"Bollocks!" she sniggers. "At Sam's party, it was as obvious as a fart in a lift that you two had something going on. And after I met her yesterday for coffee, our little chat, it just confirmed it."

I sigh, realising that my attempts at avoiding the subject are futile.

"Your guess is as good as mine. We got on so well at your wedding. In fact, we spent most evenings together."

"And nights," Amy interrupts with a smug look on her face. I neither confirm nor deny.

"We both agreed to carry on seeing each other, calling, texting and when she got home, everything was going great. Then one minute she's telling me she can't wait to see me, the next." I take a couple of deep breaths before I continue. "She called the whole thing off."

"What did you do, Cade?"

"Nothing, absolutely nothing," I gasp. "If I knew, I could at least… What did she say, anyway?"

"Nothing. Deny, deny, deny. She wouldn't budge an inch. Kept changing the subject."

"But you said…"

"I said I'd spoken to her. The fact that she wouldn't talk,

confirmed my suspicions about you two."

Silence fell between us, and I welcomed it. But it was short-lived.

"She's changed," Amy blurts out.

"In what way?"

"She's not her bubbly self. At first, I thought it was because of her mum and the stress of flying backward and forward from Bratislava, but I'm not so sure."

"She's living back here now?" I can't believe I didn't know. Then again, the only time I've actually seen her, as soon as I got near, she ran. "How often does she go back?"

"At a guess, a couple of times a month at least. I'm surprised she hasn't got shares in Ryanair. Must cost her a bloody fortune."

"That's crazy. So, is her mum still sick?"

"Not sure. Come to think of it, she's a bit cagey about that too. Oh, you need to come off here." she waves her hand, pointing to the next exit.

She continues with the direction, then tells me to pull up so she can take over the driving.

"Isaac will shit a brick if he sees you driving it into the carpark. Best keep him in the dark," she whispers, as if he'd be able to hear her.

Once we arrive at the offices and park up, we both enter the building, Amy walking slightly in front. When we get to the top of the stairs, she veers off to the right, in the opposite direction of Isaac's office.

"Where are you going?" I ask.

"To see Kat," she waves at me over her shoulder, without turning around. "I'm going to find out what's going on with Petra."

While I walk down the corridor towards Isaac's office, my thoughts and emotions are a mix of concern, uncertainty, and downright annoyance. If Petra had only talked to me, told me about her mother, then I could have done something. Don't know what, but something, maybe. Why did she come back to Bath if it meant traveling backwards and forwards to home so much?

Why did she run? I remember how her body quivered, the flush of arousal, how her pupils dilated. Was she scared of what could be if she'd given it a chance? But why?

It might have meant nothing to her, but that's not how it felt for me. Sure, I wasn't looking for anything other than a few nights of fun, but the more time I spent with her… it became more than that. When I was holding her, fucking her, both of us coming together, it was so much more than that. It's so different from with other women I've been with. With her, I felt a closeness, a connection.

I hammer on Isaac's door hard, because now I'm pissed and not in the best of moods. The door flies open. Isaac stands before me, a scowl on his face matching the one that's undoubtedly plastered across my face.

"What the fuck, Cade? It's a door, not a fucking punch bag, you douche," he roars. "Come in and sit down. If this mood of yours has anything to do with my wife, if you've upset her, I'll kick your ass. She's pregnant, you asshole."

"Fuck you Isaac, do you really have such a low opinion of me? You honestly think I'd do anything intentionally or otherwise to upset Amy, pregnant or not pregnant? If you must know, we get along fine. I really like her."

Isaac rubs the back of his neck, something he tends to do when he's trying to calm himself down. Despite our strained greeting, we still do the man hug thing before he walks to the other side of his large dark wood desk. I drop into the seat opposite him, and he slips into his own seat.

"What's going on, Cade?"

I open my mouth, but nothing comes out, so I close it again. I don't want to lie to him, so I toy with the idea of coming clean, not that I really want to do that either. I go to speak again, but stop when Isaac does instead.

"I know you've been drinking far too much, fucking around and Jesus Christ Cade, the size of you. I'm all for keeping yourself fit and all, but man, I think you need to slow down a little." I had been hitting the gym pretty hard, but I hadn't really taken much notice of how much muscle gain I'd achieved.

"Don't tell me; Ben's been spouting his mouth off again?" I tut. "You shouldn't believe everything he says."

"Ben's not a liar, and you know that," he says curtly. Isaac lets out a long sigh before continuing with the conversation. A conversation that I don't really want to be the subject of. "He's worried about you Cade, and so am I. You've got a stick up your ass the size of the Empire State Building and I want to know what's put it there." I honour him with one of my best dark looks, but all I get in return is genuine concern. "It's something to do with Petra, isn't it?"

I know I'm busted. So, I relent and tell him everything.

As I get to relay what happened at Sam's party, Isaac's desk phone rings.

"What's up." He glances at me, then swivels his chair

around so he has his back to me. "Okay, but why?" I sit and wait. "I don't understand. Okay, okay. Of course, I trust you. Bye."

"Problem?"

"Can I ask you one thing, Cade; do you really like her?" I run my fingers through my hair and avoid eye contact. "Cade, do you fucking love her?" My eyes snap to his, not only because of the sharp tone of his voice, but because he's said the one thing that I had been telling myself wasn't possible.

"How can it be love when I've spent so little time with her?"

"Shit, Cade, you've got a lot to learn. It's not about time, it's about how you feel in here," he stabs a finger to his chest. "I think I knew the first time I kissed Amy. It was like she had cast a spell over me that turned me into a love-sick puppy."

"But it's different. Amy wanted you too, while Petra pushes me away."

"Don't you believe it, brother; it wasn't as easy as that. I had to fight for her, do everything that was in my power. Hell, I even bought this fucking company so I could get her back into my life."

"So, what should I do?"

"If you want her, you go get her. If not, you walk away."

"I want her," I admit. Not only to Isaac but also to myself.

"Then stop being a pussy and man up!" he growls back. "You get your sorry ass on the next plane to Bratislava, find your girl and don't take no for an answer."

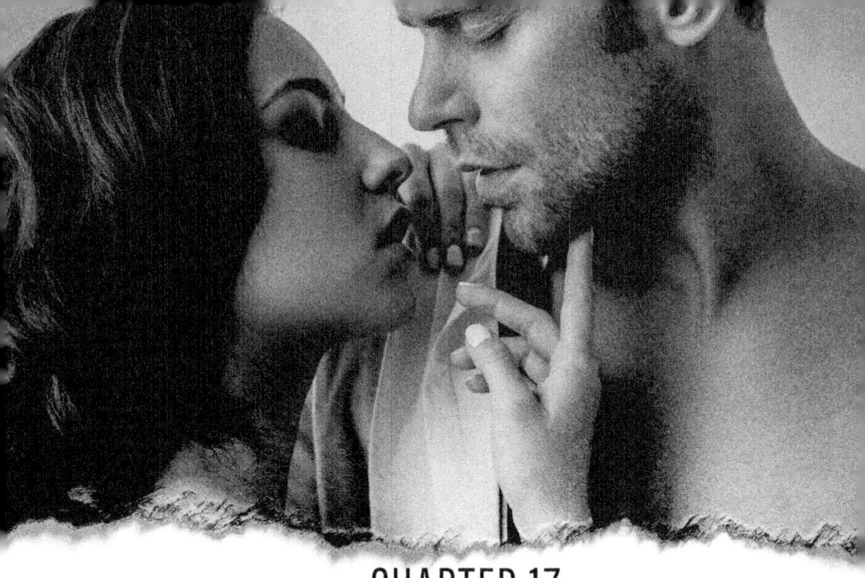

CHAPTER 17

Petra

I feel a soft hand caress the back of my head. I push slightly against it, relishing the sign of affection.

"Ty si plakala (You've been crying)," my mother whispers.

"Nie mami, len mam cervene oci od unavy (No mamma, my eyes are just red because I'm tired)."

"Neklam mi Petra, pocula som ta minulu noc zlatko. Je to kvoli tomu muzovi? (Don't lie to me Petra, I heard you last night, honey. Is it because of this man?)"

"Mami, nechcem o tom hovorit (Mamma, I don't want to talk about it)."

"Ale music o tom hovorit. Tvoje srdce sa lame pred mojimi ocami a strasne ma to boli takto ta vidiet (But you need to talk about it. Your heart is breaking right in front of my eyes, and it hurts me to see you in so much pain)."

"Mami, prosim ta. Nemozem o tom s tebou diskutovat. Nebudem o tom s tebou diskutovat (Mamma, please. I can't discuss this. I won't discuss this)."

"Tak co budes robit Petra? Budes pokracovat takto dalej? Chces sa priviest do skoreho hrobu? (So, what are you going to do, Petra? Carry on like this? Put yourself into an early grave?)" My mother never shouts, but this is as close to it as she ever gets. "Nikdy som si nemyslela ze ti takto budem kazat, ale si sebecka a hlupa (I never thought I would have to preach to you Petra, but you are being selfish and stupid)."

Her words are more painful than a physical slap to my face. I think I would have preferred that. I can't do this. I can't sit in the same room and have my mother look at me this way.

"Idem von (I'm going out)," I snap back, jumping out of my seat.

"Kam ides? (Where are you going?)"

"Potrebujem ist na vzduch (I need to get some air)."

"Ides naozaj iba na vzduch? Alebo zase utekas (Is that really what you're doing Petra? Or are you running away again?)"

"Mami? (Mamma?)" I choke out the word.

"Chod sa prejst Petra a kym sa prechadzas rozmyslaj. Zamysli sa nad tym co robis a ktorym smerom sa chces dalej poberat. Pretoze kym sa zbadas, cas ubehne a bude neskoro (Go for a walk Petra, and while you're walking, think. Think about what you are doing and where you want to go. Because before you know it, too much time will have passed and it will be too late)."

I grab my jacket from the coat peg on my way out, slamming the door as I leave.

My mother is right. However, how do you decide on your future when you have no idea what it is you want?

They say that life is a selection of pathways, each one leading in a different direction. You have a starting point, that is guaranteed. But then it's up to you which path you take. When you get to the end, there is another set, then another, until you reach your ultimate destination. Whether the road is smooth as silk or as rocky as a mountain trail, it's simply down to fate.

I call bullshit!

I didn't see any roads; I didn't get any choices. Things just happened, and I had no option but to roll with it.

I keep walking, no actual idea of where I'm going or where I want to be. How ironic, just like in my life.

By the time I get into the centre of the town, my feet hurt. So, after checking my pocket and finding a few euros, I make my way to a little café that faces out onto the main street. The smell of decadent, rich coffee hits my senses as soon as I step through the door. I quickly order at the counter, then take a seat at a small round table near the window.

I'm so lost in my thoughts that I jump when the server places the steaming cup in front of me. He utters a quick apology for scaring me before backing away.

I'm sure I look a sight. Swollen eyes, red nose and blotchy skin from all the crying. Slept in clothes and hair that hasn't seen a brush or comb since I got here. The house was empty when I first arrived here back in Bratislava, so

I collapsed on my bed and let my emotions spill out. My whole body and mind exhausted. Eventually, I had drifted off to sleep, albeit broken and disturbed. When I did wake, my face was wet with tears and I had a stress headache from hell. All I had wanted was a strong cup of black coffee before I needed to put on my happy face, but my mother had interrupted my plans.

I glance aimlessly through the window, not really focusing on anything in particular, a blurred, vaguely familiar figure catches my eye. The glass is missed up from the heat inside the café, so I wipe it with my jacket sleeve. I push my face nearer to the window for a clearer view, only to find nothing. I laugh at myself, a laugh that is close to hysteria when I realise that I'm so messed up that I'm imagining things. Deciding that I really need to get my shit together. I take a great big gulp from my cup, open a newspaper that's been left on the table, probably by a previous customer, and catch up on the latest Slovakia news.

Cade

All I seem to have done for the last 24 hours is sit in an airport, a car or a fucking plane.

After checking the flights, I'd found the next flight that I could meet would be the 13.25 flight out of Heathrow, flying via Prague. If that wasn't bad enough, it was nearly two thousand dollars, and that was for coach. I didn't care. Once I'd made up my mind, I wanted to get there as quickly as I could. Isaac had dropped everything and the next minute we were back in the Aston Martin, hot tailing it back to Heathrow.

So, here I am, after eventually arriving at Bratislava airport, now sat in a cab, heading to the address that Isaac had sent to my phone.

The cab pulls up outside a pale-yellow two-storey house, nestled between only a handful of other homes of various pastel colours. It's nothing like the other characterless apartment blocks that seem to dominate the skyline. This is a much older property, undoubtedly built well before the communism era and has been well looked after. It holds a certain quaintness and charm. An antique diamond amongst the rough, hard stone of modern monstrosities.

On paying the cab with the euros I'd hurriedly exchanged before leaving London, I step out of the car and walk up to the front door.

I hesitate for a moment, a nervousness bubbling within me. Can I take another rejection? Could I live with myself if at least I don't try? The latter being a definite no; I step forward.

I lift the ornate door knocker and bang it down, repeating the movement twice more.

I hear the muffled sound of movement behind the door, a soft recognisable voice muttering words I don't understand, brings a hesitant grin to my face. When the door opens, it's not Petra I see standing there, but an older woman.

"Dobry den, mozem vam pomoct (can I help you)?" I don't understand a word that she says, so I say the only thing I can.

"Petra? I'm looking." I point to my eyes, then realise it's a dork move, drop my hand back to my side. "Petra?"

"Petra, ano, ano. (yes, yes)" She steps back from the door and waves me in. "American?" her eyebrows rise in question. With that reaction, I guess that she's already aware of 'The American' that has been present in her daughter's life. Which can only mean that I'm at the right place.

"Thank you," I nod as I'm not sure what else to do, and step into the house. Closing the door, she gestures for me to follow her into the kitchen. When she points to one of the chairs tucked under a solid wood table, I pull it back and sit. Moving around the kitchen, I watch her as she fills a coffee machine with water and switches it on. It's one of those modern espresso machines and it looks a little out of place against the other, more dated, kitchen appliances out on the countertops.

"Kavu?" she shakes her head before saying with a smile, "Coffee?" The accent is clear, and it's apparent that her English is limited but the smile; this lady is undoubtedly Petra's mother.

"Yes," I nod back at her, with a grin, "Yes, please."

No words pass between us, only smiles and gestures except for when I offer her my hand in greeting and I introduce myself as Cade.

"Anicka," she offers in return.

After placing the small cup of black coffee in front of me, she stands for a while, smiling and observing.

"Ste velmi pekny muz (you are a very handsome man)." Her expression clearly indicating that whatever she is saying, it's a positive comment. Before I have time to make any kind of response, not that I'd know what response to give, she walks out of the room.

Left by myself, I look around the room. It's simple, clean and what seems to be old traditional.

At the sound of soft speaking, I turn to find Anicka walking back into the kitchen. Stood beside her is a tiny child, at a guess, by the way she is unsteady on her feet, about twelve to eighteen months old. As she gets nearer, I can see that her skin is the same olive shade as Anicka's, her tiny full lips and nose a miniature version of Petra's. Her hair is dark brown, but even at this distance, it looks like it's been woven with shiny golden threads. But what stands out the most is her beautiful eyes, that are the perfect shade of blue.

"Mami (mamma)," a voice calls from the hallway. "Prepac (I am sorry)."

Completely distracted by the baby girl, I hadn't heard the front door open.

Petra comes into the room, but is stopped dead in her tracks. Her eyes flit from me, to the child, to her mother, before words rapidly fire from her mouth.

"Mami, co to do kelu robis (Mum, what the hell were you thinking)?" She steps forward and picks up the baby and holds her tightly to her chest. The baby giggles, grasping onto the fabric of Petra's top with her tiny hands. When pushing her face into the crook of Petra's neck, Petra places a kiss on the top of her head. The sight is a little surreal, yet it tugs on my heart as I watch her eyes close, lips lingering on the young child's head; unconditional love at its purest.

"She's mine, isn't she?" I blurt without a second thought

about the consequences.

For a moment, I think she's going to deny it. The atmosphere in the room almost stifling. When she speaks, it's clear and precise.

"Yes Cade, you're her father."

"What the fuck, Petra," I shout. The chair legs scrape across the floor, making a loud irritating noise, one that I take little notice of but the baby does, and lets out a high pitch squeal before bursting into tears.

"Shh!" Petra coos, as she rocks and comforts the upset child. I take a step towards them, but the fierce shake of her head stops me dead in my tracks. "Mami, vezmi ju (Mum, take her)," she hands the baby to her mother, who then takes her out of the room. "How dare you shout and swear like that in front of my child?"

"Don't you mean our child?" I counter with less volume but more venom. "Shit Petra, how could you have kept this from me?" I pace the floor, my hands gripping great handfuls of my hair, as the enormity of this revelation sinks in. "So, that's why you ran, because you couldn't look me in the face, while keeping this a secret from me." I step up to her, so I'm close enough that she can feel and hear the anger that radiates from me. "Did you get a kick out of it? Did you enjoy playing your deceitful little game? Trouble is Petra, liars and cheats always get found out."

"It wasn't like that,"

"So, tell me what was it like?" I almost spit in her face.

"I… I…"

"What's the matter Petra, can't think up another lie quick enough?" I'm right up in her face, and I can see fear in her eyes. I need to calm down before I do something stupid. "I need to get out of here." I push past her, making my way to leave. When I get to the front door, I look back only to see her stood at the other end of the corridor. Even at this distance, I can see the devastation on her face. My heart tells me to go to her, but my head tells me otherwise. "This isn't over, Petra; this isn't over by a long shot." I turn my back on her and leave.

Petra

As the door slams, I drop to my knees and give way to yet more tears. This is a different kind of hurt. My own selfish pity had fuelled the previous pain. My lost chances, my insecure future, my heartache. This, this was his pain, a future that has been forced upon him. A life that he didn't want. But most of all, the hurt from my deceit.

When the last strangled sob escapes me, all cried out, I swipe the tears from both my eyes and take a long, deep breath. Holding onto the wall, I ease myself to my feet and walk back into the kitchen and move around the room in a dazed like state. I pick up the cup that he used and run my finger around the rim, touching the very spot where his lips had been. I take it to the sink and place it carefully to the side. The chair where he sat is still pushed out from the table where he had risen, along with his anger. I let my hands flit across the back, before lifting and placing it back under. Turning on the hot tap, I squeeze a little, washing up liquid into the water stream as it gushes into the sink. I wash the cup, the spoon, and a couple of other leftover items in the hot soapy water. I pop some of the sudsy bubbles with the tip of my finger, listening to the crackle as they burst. But my resolve eventually shatters, and I find myself yet again, flooded with emotion as I hold tight onto the edge of the counter, the only thing that's keeping me upright.

"Petra," my mum whispers as she wraps her arms around me. I let my head drop back onto her shoulder as my body wracks with sobs.

"Viktoria?" I ask once my tears subside. I turn to face her.

"Spi (She's sleeping)." She cups my face and kisses my cheek. I slide my arms around her waist and move into her ever open and inviting arms. How she holds me, takes me back to when I was a small child. When we would sit for hours cuddling and watching TV re-runs of Arabela, stories of the fairy-tale princess with a magic ring, who falls for a boy in the real world. Even Arabela's magical life wasn't that straightforward. I'm so lucky to have my mum and the love that she extends unconditionally to both me and my child.

"Chod si k nej lahnut, aby si tam bola, ked sa prebudi. Chybas jej. (Go lay with her so you are there when she wakes. She misses you)." The smile and nod I give her are barely identifiable, but I'm emotionally exhausted, and it's all I can give. I leave and make my way upstairs.

CHAPTER 18

Petra

My abrupt awakening is because of a tiny hand slapping at my face, and when I open my eyes, I see the most angelic little face with the brightest of eyes and the cutest of smiles. The giggle that goes along with it has my heart fluttering with the type of love and joy that only a child can provoke.

"Hi there, baby girl," I coo and pop her nose gently with my finger before placing a hundred and one kisses on her beautiful face. "Mummy's missed you so much," I punctuate each word with a kiss. She wriggles and giggles as I add a tickle or two.

Playtime gets interrupted by a knock on the door. My mum gives me an apologetic look and at first, I think that it's because she's disturbed our time together, but when she hands me my phone, I realise that's not the case.

The phone is lit up but not making a sound, so I know that it's a call and it's live. Cade's name shows on the screen. I give my mum a dirty look, shaking my head, wondering why the hell she answered it? With trepidation, I hold the phone to my ear, bracing myself for what God only knows might come next.

"Hello?"

"We need to talk."

"Then talk, but make it quick. I'm busy."

"Well shit, Petra, get un-busy because I think this is a little more important, don't you? You know, the fact that I have a child that I didn't have a damn clue about. That because of you, I've missed the chance of spending time with her in the first months of her life, something that I can never get back."

I don't reply. To be honest, I don't know what to say in my defence.

I don't need to see him to know that he's probably got his hand in his hair. The deep sigh I hear only highlights the fact that he's trying to regain a modicum of composure.

"Can you meet me?" his voice is now softer but laced with a hint of desperation.

"Where are you?" I ask.

"I'm at a hotel. It's the," I hear him shuffling papers around, "The Radisson Blue, near the National Theatre."

"The Carton. I know where that is."

"Will you bring her with you? God," he huffs, "I don't even know my child's name."

"No!" I snap. "I'm not bringing my child into what will

probably end up being a screaming match, Cade. I won't have her subjected to that."

"Petra," the sound of my name, in his deep voice, sends a splattering of goose bumps across my skin. "I'm sorry. I never meant to upset her. Why do you think I left when I did? I needed time to get my head around this, time to cool down. When I came here looking for you, the last thing I expected was to find out that I'm a dad."

Silence falls between us, giving me time to mull over his request.

"One hour. I'll meet you in one hour. But not at the hotel." The last thing I need right now is to be in a closed environment with him. It needs to be somewhere open; public. Somewhere both of us will have to hold our tongues and control our tempers. "When you come out of the hotel, turn right, walk towards the Danube River until you get to the promenade and I'll meet you there."

"Please bring her with you. No shouting, only talking. I promise."

"Okay. I'll see you there in one hour."

"I'll be there." The determination in his voice leaves me with no doubt.

"Cade,"

"Yes?"

"Viktoria, her name's Viktoria."

CHAPTER 19

Cade

I'm on time, but she's early.

It gives me the opportunity to look at her from afar as I approach where she is standing.

I watch as she's crouched down at the side of the stroller where Viktoria is sitting.

Viktoria; my daughter, my child.

That fact still has my head in a spin, but I also feel a sense of attainment, excited, albeit scared of this extra responsibility in my life.

Petra's hand stretches out, pointing to something in the distance. The light breeze plays with her hair, flipping it across her face. She tips her head to one side until the wind picks it up and flicks it away again. The jeans that she's wearing are a faded blue and fit her ass perfectly. As she straightens up, I can see that there is a small tear with frayed edges below her ass cheek. At first, I think that the yellow tee that's she wearing is worn loose, but then I realise that I'd seen her wearing it before. Then it had hugged her body. She's lost weight. I can't believe I didn't notice before. It's undoubtedly because of the stress and pressure that she must have been under for the past months. A bolt of guilt hits me, along with an underlying annoyance. If I'd have known, I could have been there for her.

When I get a few feet away from her, she catches sight of me from the corner of her eye. She turns to face me; I can read her expression. It screams fear and anxiety, mixed up with a shitload of defiance. Her body language has morphed from relaxed mother interacting with her child to a woman who has built a barricade in order to protect herself. To protect herself from me. But we can't have that now, can we? Not if I want to reach my goal. The reason I'm here in the first place. Her recent revelation, does nothing to deter me.

I know I need to tread carefully, but I also need answers to the questions that are driving me insane.

"Hi." Placing my hand on her upper arm, I lean in and place a gentle kiss on her cheek. Her body stiffens at my touch and her reaction hurts me more than I'd like to admit to. Moving to the front of the stroller, I hunker down so I'm face to face with my daughter, my child, Viktoria. "Hi there, Viktoria," I run my index finger across the back of her tiny hand. "How are you today?" She giggles and wriggles in response, so much that if she wasn't belted into the seat, she'd be out of there. The smile she gives me comes with four pearly white teeth, two up and two down, along with a little dimple on each cheek. "How about we go for a walk while I talk to your mamma?" Again, I'm greeted with the same response. I know she understands basic words, maybe a little more, but she probably doesn't really understand what I'm saying to her or the drama that's going on around her. However, I know that at this age they are like sponges, learning and absorbing new words, skills and reactions all the time. At least that's what Google said when I did some research, before I left the hotel.

I stand straight and glance over at Petra. Wide eyed, mouth open, her expression tells me that my actions were not what she expected. It's like a punch to the gut that she thinks so little of me.

"Hi again," I give her a tentative smile.

"Hi," she mumbles, still a little dazed.

"Shall we?" I ask, holding my hand out I invite her to lead the way in our walk, letting her decide which direction to take. Once she makes her move, I step into place beside her. It takes a few minutes for her to speak, but however many questions I have simmering on my tongue, I want it to be her that makes the first move.

"How's the hotel?" Her line of question doesn't surprise me. I haven't forgotten her obsession with hotel rooms and their décor. Although, I suspect that the small talk is a way of avoiding the inevitable hot topic.

"It's good. Do you want to come and look?"

"No, thank you. I've seen them many times before."

"Really?" I give her a questionable look.

"I've worked there in the past."

Silence.

"Did you pick that hotel because it was near to the American Embassy, or was that a fluke?"

"The Embassy is near?" I say with a straight face.

"Cade, you can't tell me you didn't see the American flag flying outside." The smallest of smiles adorns her face, so subtle that most people would miss it.

"I admit, when I left your house, I asked for directions to the Embassy."

"And why would you do that?" she scowls at me, her walls becoming thicker by the minute. "What are you planning to do, Cade? I don't care how good a lawyer you are. If you think that you can take her away from me, I'll fight you all the way. All the f…" she stops the word that was close to falling from her mouth, her eyes falling to the child, in the stroller in front of her, before finishing her sentence. "All the way."

"Petra, I went to the Embassy because the chances are that there would be a decent hotel nearby. I have no intentions of taking Viktoria away from you." I can see that she is visibly shaking, so when we come to a park bench, I stop and gesture for her to sit. She takes a seat once she positions the stroller, so Viktoria is looking out towards the river. I sit beside her, close enough so I can talk quietly, but not close enough to make her uncomfortable. "When I left, I was crazy mad, and I needed time to think. Petra, I'd found out that I'm a dad, the last thing I expected when I came looking for you. It blew my mind."

"Why did you come looking for me?"

"Don't you think it should be me that gets to ask the questions?" I reply, my eyebrow raised. She tries to give off an air of confidence, but the way she shuffles uncomfortably in her seat, tells me a different story. Then she straightens her back, sits upright, with her hands gripping the seat at each side of her knees, before she finally speaks with a weak attempt at strength and determination.

"Okay, so what do you want to know, Cade?"

"Did you know you were pregnant when you called it off?"

"Yes."

"But you said you were okay, that you were on the pill."

"Yeah! But apparently being travel sick, then throwing up after a shit load of champagne the very next day, can, as my doctor had great pleasure in telling me," she air quotes, "reduce the level of protection and reliability of your contraceptive pill."

"Then why didn't you tell me, instead of lying and feeding me all that bullshit?" I keep the volume and tone of my voice as steady as possible, considering the emotion raging within me.

"Because it was clear that was the last thing you wanted to be stuck with." This time it was her that was shouting. The stroller moved suddenly as a cry rang out. Instantly, she was on her feet, moving around to the front to comfort Viktoria. "Hush baby, it's okay." She strokes the side of the little girl's face before placing a handful of peppered kisses along her forehead. "Mummy's sorry for shouting. It's okay." Unfastening the belt, she lifts her out of the stroller seat and brings her to sit on her knee.

Viktoria looks at me with big tear-filled eyes, and I melt.

"How could you be so sure, when you didn't even give

me the curtesy to choose?" I speak quietly, so not to upset the now nearly settled child. With my index finger, I go to stroke the back of her hand, but she reaches out and grabs it, wrapping her tiny fist around it.

"I heard you talking to Isaac and Ben, the morning after the wedding." My confused expression prompts her to continue. "What was it you said now?" she taps her finger on her chin in an exaggerated way, while holding tight to Viktoria. Her arm wrapped around her waist, holding her firmly on her lap. "You're well and truly trapped this time. Ball, chain and another kid on the way. Oh, yes, and what was the other thing you said… 'Rather you than me, brother. You're well and truly pussy whipped this time.'"

"I was winding my brother up."

"Really?" she sniggers, "What about when you were talking about the case you lost. You made it pretty clear that you were glad that you didn't have the responsibility of a family and kids."

"I was, at the time," I exhale. "Look, I never wanted to have a serious relationship. Marriage, kids and the commitment that comes with it."

"What, so I should have told you so you could reject me, make me look like a stupid, naïve woman who should know better?" She makes to stand, but the gentle pressure of my hand on her arms stops her and she drops back onto the bench.

"That was then. This is now, Petra."

"So, what changed your mind? Just because you got me pregnant, doesn't mean you can change your mind like the flick of a switch." She looks me in the eye, something she's done very little of since we started this tense conversation. "It's not a game, Cade. It's not like you can play the doting parent when it suits you. It's a lifetime commitment."

"If that's the case, then why are you leaving her here while you fly back to Bath?" As soon as the words leave me, I'm full of remorse. The painful look on her face does nothing but intensify it. "I'm sorry. I didn't mean that."

"If you must know, I go back to Bath every Sunday night, so at least I have a job with decent money. Don't you think I tried to get work here? I'm sick to death of filling out application forms, trying to get a job with decent pay. But as soon as they find out I have a baby, then miraculously they have someone more," she makes another air quote, this time one-handed, "suitable for the job." She puts on her best fake smile as she looks down at her child. Moving Viktoria to the ground, so her little shoes hit the floor, I watch as Petra holds her hand to help support her stance. "But I continue to try, do you know why?" her head tilts forward and a single tear hits the fabric covering her knee.

"Because every Sunday when I leave to catch that plane, my heart is left behind." The pitch of her voice is high and the last few words are cracked. The tears come more readily now and I can't stop myself from reaching out to her. Before my hand makes contact, she halts me with her free hand.

"So, don't think for one minute that I leave her because I want to. I do it because I have to." As I'm about to say my piece, Viktoria reaches her hands up to be lifted. I sit for a moment, unsure at first, but then elation takes its place when I realise she's reaching up to me. I quickly glance at Petra, and she gives me a nod of approval. I bring Viktoria up and on to my knee, her face turned towards me, constantly watching. Laying her palm flat against my cheek, I can feel the softness of her skin as she holds it there. The angelic smile that lights up her face, the sparkle that dances in her eyes, has me swallowing hard to hold down the emotion that is fighting to escape.

"Hello Viktoria." She giggles and throws her head back. The sudden movement and the fear that she may fall, has me wrapping my arms around her and pulling her close to my chest. Petra laughs at my obvious fear, at which Viktoria joins in with her sweet little giggle.

"Hey! That's not funny. I thought I was going to drop her."

"Cade, relax," she rubs my upper arm. "She's fine."

Viktoria snuggles against my chest, her hands clutching the fabric at the shoulders of my jacket. The warmth that radiates through me from her closeness fuels the build-up of the unconditional love that I undoubtedly feel for my daughter. My daughter, my blood, my life.

"You changed my mind," I say with clarity. "Before, you asked me what changed my mind, Petra. It was you."

"I don't understand," she gasps out.

"You're right, you are absolutely right. I wasn't looking for a wife, a family. Hell, I didn't even want a girlfriend. But when I met you, you changed everything. Your sass, exceptional wit and your strength is so incredibly sexy, drawing me in, making me want to spend every moment with you. When I saw your vulnerable side, that flash of fear in your eyes, I wanted to protect you, shield you from everything that might cause you pain. Find the reason why your fear existed and eliminate it so I never see it adorn that beautiful face again." I stop and take a breath. Considering I'm a lawyer who has to be articulate and precise when putting the point across, I'm finding it damn hard to express myself. "You fired a spark in me that made me want all that, but only if I could have it with you."

"Cade, I…"

"I know," I interrupt her, something I wouldn't get away with in court. "We've hardly spent any time together. We still have a lot to find out about each other, but I want this, Petra. I've been an absolute jackass since you put a stop to us. I've been drifting, lost even, but I want to be grounded. I want you and Viktoria to be in my life, permanently."

"Cade…",

"Look, I'm going to take Viktoria over there," I point to the small vendor's cart selling sodas and ice-creams. "Get her an ice-cream, give you a chance to, well think about what I've just said. Do you want anything?" She shakes her head in response. "Okay. Come on sweetheart," I stand, holding Viktoria tightly in my arms and walk over to the vendor, leaving before Petra even gets the chance to reject me again. The thought that she will, well, it damn near kills me.

Petra

I wipe the tears from my face with the back of my hand, as I watch Cade carry Viktoria. Her arm wraps around his neck and she looks straight at him, a toothy grin on her face.

She's absolutely fascinated by him.

With his head turns towards her, I can see his mouth moving as he chats to her, a definitive lift to the corners as he smiles. Even at this distance, I can see the light in his eyes that can only be described as adoration. The profound and powerful connection between them does not elude me. In fact, it provokes yet more inarguable feelings towards him.

Viktoria does her usual giggle and wiggle, but this time Cade is ready for it, and keeps a firm hold.

Shit, shit, shit. Looks like I'm not the only one he's bewitched, with his American cowboy good looks and irresistible charm.

Cade hands over an ice cream cone that's way too big for Viktoria's tiny little hands, so he folds his hand around hers to give it support. When she puts her mouth to the creamy topping, she wrinkles her nose as the coldness hits her lips. A white blob now decorates the tip of her nose and Cade uses his thumb to wipe it away. As Viktoria licks one side of the cone, Cade licks at the other. I'm guessing to control the already dripping liquid that's threatening to hit his shirt, rather than his own need for ice-cream.

While watching, the unprecedented interaction between the two of them pierces me. A knot in my stomach starts off small, only to become bigger and bigger, slowly rising into my chest. A consuming sense of remorse saturates my very being. I hold it in as tight as I can, but the barriers are unstable. The wall begins to crumble.

Cade puts Viktoria back into the pushchair, a large smear of ice-cream across the shoulder of his jacket. Bending, he fiddles about for what seems like a lifetime, strapping Viktoria in securely. I know I should help, but I'm frozen to the spot. I hear the click of the catch before Cade stands upright before me.

"I'm so sorry, Cade," the words a little mumble between the sobs and uncontrollable tears. "I'm so fucking sorry."

"Hey, hey," he comes to me and this time when he touches me, I fall into him. His arms envelope me and instantly I feel his warmth seep into my very soul. "What's all this?"

"I've been such a bitch. I was wrong to keep this from you." I try to control the body shakes that I'm having, but my emotional defences have come crashing down. "I'm so sorry. I thought it was for the best, truly I did."

"I can't believe it didn't get back to me through Amy." The way his hand runs across my back is soothing, but my emotions still rage on.

"Amy doesn't know. Kat has known for a while. She guessed something was up, and eventually, with her persistent and annoying questioning, she eventually got it out of me. I made her swear on the life of Ronald McDonald not to tell anyone."

"That's strange," he utters to himself.

"Why? Because Ronald McDonald's not even real? Shh! Don't tell Kat that." I give him a weak smile.

"No, not that," he smiles back, both of our moods lightening a little from my weak attempt at humour.

"What is?" I look up at him, my tears subsiding.

"Isaac. He was very adamant that I should get on that plane to come here. Especially after he'd just come off the phone with Amy." The corner of his mouth turns up at one side. "Your secret might be already out."

"Oh my God, Cade. What if everyone knows that I've had a baby, your baby?"

"Is that such a bad thing?" I don't miss the hurt look that cloaks his face.

"Sleeping with the boss's brother? Getting pregnant with him within a matter of hours?" I pull away from his protective embrace. "I know exactly what people will think. They'll think that I did it to trap you, that I'm a gold-digger."

"Let them," he sniggers as he pulls me back against his firm body. "Petra, you kept it a secret, from me, from everyone. If you had been trying to entrap me, then you would have been shouting it loud and proud, not struggling to get through it, all by yourself."

"I have my mum."

"And your mum is wonderful. But I almost wish you had been out to trap me because I would have undoubtedly won you over, got you to fall helplessly in love with me." He gives me one of his cocky smiles.

"You're so full of yourself." I slap his chest with my hand, but he catches and holds it there. I'm unable to hide a gentle smile. "Cade, I'm…"

"Shh!" his finger across my lips stops me from finishing what I'm about to say. I tilt my head up towards him, looking into his eyes, I see the heat building within them. When he pulls me even closer, face to face, I can feel and smell his soft, minty breath. We're so close now that I ache for the feel of his lips on mine. Just as they are about to touch, Viktoria cries out 'Mami' which has us both pulling apart, making me realise how quickly Cade has slipped into the role of parent.

Turning my attention to Viktoria, I find her holding a rather soggy cone in one hand and her mouth and cheeks are covered in the melted ice-cream. A trail of the same stickiness runs from her chin to halfway down her coat. Her big blue eyes, the double of Cade's, look back at me.

"Hey, baby girl, did you enjoy that?" she greets me with a gigantic smile that makes my heart soar. As always. "I think we better go home and get you cleaned up."

I wipe the worst of the mess up with baby wipes I have tucked in the pushchair's hood. Then stand to address Cade.

"Will you meet me for dinner tonight? We still have a lot to talk about," he asks before I even have a chance to speak.

"Mhm!" I reply with a nod. Suddenly, the thought of us going on what I can only describe as a date has me feeling heady and giddy all at once.

"I'll come and pick you up about seven?"

"Can we make it a little later so I can bath Viktoria and put her to bed? It's important to me. It's the one thing I miss the most when I'm not here."

"Of course."

"Why don't I meet you outside your hotel at eight? There's a really nice Italian restaurant a short walk away. If I remember rightly, you do like Italian."

"Perfect," he replies with a smile. "Why don't you walk back to the hotel with me now and I can get the concierge to call you a cab?"

"It's fine, it's not that far, we can walk."

"Petra, please let me call you a cab. I know it must exhaust you with the travelling back and forth. Besides, then I'll know you've both got home safely."

"Okay, I guess I am a little tired." My heightened emotions over the past few hours haven't helped with my fatigue.

We walk in silence but it's a comfortable one, both of us casting the occasional glance at each other, always accompanied with a smile. It's surreal. We both are acting like two high school kids, silently flirting with each other. It's kind of cute and does nothing to dampen my giddiness.

Cade disappears into the hotel to speak to the concierge, so I check on Viktoria while I wait for his return. She's fast asleep, which is a surprise after the sugary treat that I feared might send her into hyper mode. Then again, most of it did go down her clothing and not actually in her mouth.

"It should be here in two or three minutes," Cade announces when he comes to stand beside me. "Damn, she's so beautiful," he sighs as he watches his daughter sleeping. He turns to look at me. "Just like her mamma."

Holy Jesus, I'm sure my heart skips a beat before doing a triple somersault landing firmly on its knees. If a heart had knees, that is. I want to say something but other than, fuck me gorgeous, loud and proud, in the middle of a relatively busy street, I'm lost for words. So, I change the subject.

"I better get Viktoria out of the pushchair before the cab arrives."

"May I?" he asks, gesturing to our sleeping child.

"Yes, of course." I bend and unbuckle the safety straps that hold Viktoria in, then step back, giving Cade access. With his enormous hands and strength, he lifts her effortlessly and with such gentleness that she barely stirs. Watching as he cradles her in his powerful arms, her head resting on his shoulder as she sleeps, brings a lump to my throat. Cade's need and want to protect her is screamingly obvious. His feelings for her are crystal clear, with how his eyes shine whenever his gaze falls upon her. It's astounding how quickly he has fallen in love with her, making me wonder why I ever doubted him.

Just as I'm collapsing the pushchair, a car pulls up. The driver jumps out and quickly walks to us, takes the pushchair from me and loads it into the boot.

"You get in and I'll hand her to you."

When Viktoria is firmly snuggled in my arms, Cade leans in and places a soft kiss on to her forehead and her lips curl into a gentle smile. Coincidence or an unexplainable bond, I'm not sure, but it leaves me wondering if she's actually feigning sleep.

"I'll see you at eight." He places a firm, hard kiss on my lips before stepping back and closing the door. Slightly stupefied, my fingertips go to where his lips had been, the essence of him still lingering.

I mumble the address to the driver as he pulls away from the curb.

Wow! That was the type of kiss that holds a promise of more to come. I bloody hope so.

CHAPTER 20

Cade

It's six minutes past eight, and I'm thinking that she's not going to turn up. Was the progress that we seem to have made earlier, just my wishful thinking? Has Petra re-enforced her wall of protection in the few hours since I saw her? The sinking sensation in my gut lifts when a cab pulls up to the curb side and I catch sight of her sat in the back. I step forward to open the door at the same time as she hands over a few euros to the driver in the front.

When I hold out my hand, she takes it. The softness of her skin is a total contrast to the powerful electric sensation that comes from her touch. The energy races to every single part of my body. Every nerve, every muscle, every goddamn sensor, sending them into high alert. No woman has ever had this effect, caused this kind of reaction, had this control over me. It scares the hell out of me, but it also makes me realise she is unequivocally the one.

"Hi," is all I say as she steps out of the cab. I allow myself time to take in the full sight of her, and I can only describe it as unsurpassable. Nothing, no one, not even the most spectacular sunset on a Florida beach, could compare to the utter vision that stands before me.

The little black dress she has on is much, much more than a little black dress. The fabric skims her body like a second skin. Although she has undoubtedly lost some weight, she still has that tantalising curve that goes in from under her breast, coming out at the hip. The perfect hourglass. The criss-cross of thin straps that run over the shoulders, neckline and across the crest of her breasts, gives it a peek-a-boo effect. Now you see skin, now you don't. Classy, demure, discreet sexiness at its best, which my dick agrees with whole-heartedly as it jumps about in my dress pants.

"Stunning, you look truly stunning." I bring her further to me until we're nearly touching. Leaning forward, I kiss both her cheeks, hovering after the second and whispering softly into her ear, "You take my breath away."

The sexual tension bounces between us, but Petra quickly breaks the volley.

"Thank you," she says with a delicate cough. "The Senator is across the other side of the road, down one of the side streets." She slowly turns to walk and I follow, falling into step beside her.

"How's Viktoria?"

"Adorable, cheeky and quite a handful, but I wouldn't

have her any other way," she laughs. "In fact, that's why I'm a little late. She's normally great at bedtime, goes down straight away, but tonight of all nights, she decided to put up a fight."

"Oh, that could be my fault. The ice-cream was kinda large."

"I don't think it was that. She had a lot of excitement in one day."

"I guess. So, you were late because you didn't want to leave until she had settled?"

"Nope. I was late because once I realised I was going to be late, I let mum take care of her. When I went to give her a kiss, she was giggling and blew the biggest snot bubble you've ever seen. It popped just as she decided she wanted to give me a cuddle. It was disgusting. I had to change my top, and this was the only other thing half decent." She indicates to the dress. "Otherwise, it would have been jeans and a sweatshirt. I don't go out much, can you tell?" She points to the restaurant in front of us. "This is it."

The partially enclosed outside area was nothing special, but it looked clean and presentable with its crisp white and red colour scheme. "Would you prefer to sit inside or out?"

"Inside I think." I let her take the lead, partly because it's the gentlemanly thing to do. Mainly so I can get a good look at her from behind. The slight sway of her hips and ass is spectacular. "Remind me to thank our beautiful daughter when I see her."

"What for?" she asks over her shoulder.

"For getting you to wear that dress," I reply, the depth of my approval clearly evident in my voice.

"Ahoy, vitaj (Hello, welcome)." A guy in a suit greets us inside the doorway. "Stol pre dvoch? (Table for two)." The inside mirrors the outside somewhat with the same tables, chairs and colour scheme, but with the added elegance of grand crystal lighting and rich wall coverings.

"Ano prosim, (Yes please)" Petra responds before translating to me in English.

"Ask him for a quiet table where we can talk," I add.

I watch their facial expressions as they talk fast and fluidly in Slovak. When they laugh together and he places a hand on her arm, feelings I've rarely experienced before have me straightening my stance and my fists clenching at my sides. Jealousy, protectiveness and insecurity. Not just because the guy is over friendly towards her, but also that I can't damn well understand what he or she is saying to each other and it's making me very uneasy. The disgruntled look I flash him must hit home as he immediately escorts us to a table in a corner, away from the main area. It's about as good as it's going to get. I move swiftly, almost knocking the server off his feet, so I can get to pull the chair out for Petra to sit. The server raises his eyebrows at me, holds both of his hands up at chest level, and takes a step back. Petra shakes her head, sitting as I slowly push the chair in towards the table. I take both the menus from the outstretched hand of the server and pass one to her. She speaks to him again in Slovak. Much to my annoyance they laugh, and it's clear the joke is on me. I wait until he walks away before I speak.

"What's so funny?"

"You," she chuckles. "You're acting like an overprotective Neanderthal. What's got into you?"

"I didn't like the way he was looking at you, touching you. You're here with me and he should have been respectful of that, rather than being all over you."

"Woah!" she cocks her head and her eyebrows come together as she scowls. "Just because I'm the mother of your child, doesn't mean that you automatically have a claim over me." She looks around before leaning forward across the table. She lowers her voice before saying, "What are you going to do next? Get your dick out and start pissing all over me, marking your territory."

"Well, I'm not really into that type of thing, but if it's something that turns you on, then I'm willing to give it a try."

Her eyes go wide, her mouth gapes open, then she bursts out laughing. She's laughing so hard that I can see the tears start to collect in the corner of her eyes, as she takes huge gasps of air between each burst. Her laughter is so infectious that it draws me in too, obliterating the uneasy atmosphere.

"Damn, it's good to see the sassy, fun loving Petra that stole my heart in Florida." The words spill naturally and unrehearsed from my mouth.

Her laugher stops suddenly and again her eyes go wide and her mouth gapes open. No laughter this time as my words hit home. "Don't look so shocked. You had me hooked from the first time you called me cowboy, but my stubbornness wouldn't let me admit it to myself."

"Cade, I…"

"I want you so much Petra, you have no idea." I can see the server hovering about in my peripheral vision, but

I don't give a rat's ass. "If we weren't in a public place, I'd lay you on this table now and fuck you slow, then fast, until you're screaming for mercy." Her mouth is still agape, yet her eyes are now dark with want. "In fact, I might do it anyway, just so that douche bag of a server over there, gets my message loud and clear, to keep the hell away from you."

"He's my cousin, from my late father's side. I didn't even know he was back living in Bratislava and worked here until now."

"Oh!" It was my turn to be taken by surprise. "Why didn't you tell me?"

"You didn't give me a chance," she sniggers.

"Are you hungry?"

"Not really." There is hunger in her eyes, but the want for food is not what they're projecting.

"Come back to my hotel, I need to fuck you."

"Funny, I was thinking the same thing."

CHAPTER 21

Petra

When we fall through the door into Cade's hotel room, we are both out of breath. The speed at which we walked back here is partly to blame for our breathless state. However, the way we fall into each other as soon as the door slams behind us is the main factor.

With desperate hands, we grab and tear at each other's clothes. Our mouths only breaking contact when necessary. It's raw, it's harsh, and it's clumsy. Like a couple of thirsty, starving desperados, wanting only what the other can give. So much that we are teetering on the edge of the pit of insanity.

"I'm sorry, baby, but I can't wait. I need to be in you," he growls. His hand slides between my legs, slipping in between my folds only to return, covered in the evidence of my arousal. "You're ready for me baby, you're so fucking ready."

Pushing me back against the door, he grips my arse and lifts me. I wrap my legs around him, letting out a gasp when I feel his hard cock pushing into me.

"I've missed you so much baby, you feel so fucking good," he rasps. "Forgive me, because this is gonna be fast." The speed at which he thrusts into me is crazy, yet he still goes deep, hitting my spot every time. I'm not a come without foreplay kind of girl but holy orgasmoley, he has it, and I'm getting it.

When my orgasm hits, my body tightens around his cock and with less than a handful more of thrusts, I feel his warmth fill me as he growls out my name.

He releases his hold on my arse and lets my feet fall slowly to the ground. Our slick with sweat skin still touching as we cling to each other. He kisses me slowly. His lips are soft and sweet tasting, making me want more. As if reading my mind, he takes hold of the back of my head, bringing me nearer, kissing me deeper, making me dizzy with desire.

Cade's hand slides from behind my head, over my shoulder and down until the flat of his hand is laid over breast. "Your body is so fucking sexy," he murmurs into my mouth as he teases me, circling the palm over my nipple, already hard with arousal. I push against his hands, seeking more pressure until the pain from the friction becomes almost unbearable. A rush of heat careens towards my clit as his hand goes there too, as if to catch it. But when his expert finger finds it first time, and starts flicking, circling and pressing on the already excited spot, I moan out only to be silenced by another heated kiss.

I come on his hand.

I come in his mouth.

When I come on his cock again, this time it's slow, precise and gentle. Well, up to a point anyway, it still ends up hot and hard as we shudder together, spilling each other's names into our gasping mouths.

"Do you hate me?" I ask as we lay barely awake, exhausted from our sex session.

"Hate you? Why would I hate you?"

"Stealing away the chance for you to see the birth of your child, her first breath, her first smile, her first…" I have to stop because the pain that grips my chest from the realisation and guilt of what I have done, renders me speechless. The tears that fall don't help either. "Because I wouldn't blame you if you did," I stutter between tears.

"Petra," he rolls over onto his side and turns me too, so I have no option but to face him. "I won't pretend that it doesn't hurt, that I'm not disappointed you didn't trust me enough to tell me. But I don't hate you."

"But could you ever forgive me?"

"That, I won't lie, may take some time, but I will."

"How can you be so sure of that? How do you know that eventually it won't eat away at you, so eventually you end up hating me?"

"There is no way I could ever hate you baby, because I love you."

The words hit me hard and I wait for the panic to set in. I wait for the familiar feelings; the walls coming around me, that I mentally erect every time someone tries to get close.

My shield, my barricade. But I feel no fear.

I push away from him and sit up on the bed with my legs crossed.

"Petra?" I look back at him with wide eyes and a full heart.

"When I was fifteen, I fell in love." I say softly. "I was confident, happy, and full of life. Michal was three years older than me, so my mum wasn't happy about me seeing him, but she didn't stop me either. I guess she always gave me more freedom than the other kids got. I think she thought it had hurt me enough, losing Dad when I was so young. She'd avoid an argument at all costs."

"You don't have to explain to me," his face is shrouded with sadness.

"Yes, I do, because then you might understand." A simple nod is what I get in response.

"At first, I was the strong one in the relationship. In fact, my friends used to joke about how I had Michal wrapped around my little finger. But oh, my God, how things changed." I quickly glance at Cade and take a deep breath before I continue. "They say love is blind, well in my case, there was certainly an element of truth in that. I didn't see the lies and the cheating, the slow manipulation. I didn't see how, over the three and a half years I was with him, he gradually controlled me. He would tell me what to wear, how much to eat, then came the relentless sly digs." I let out a strangled laugh as I try to push down the emotions that were building as memories fill my head.

"Petra," Cade mumbles as he reaches out and takes my hand. Our eyes meet and I see empathy but not in a condescending way, giving me the confidence to continue.

"He was clever, oh so clever. He used to make comments about my weight, my skin, how I wore my hair. As soon as I sniped back at him, he would declare how sorry he was, that it was only a joke." I let out another deep sigh. "But it was never a joke. He was dragging me down to a point where my self-esteem was totally obliterated."

As my internal emotions build, a tear escapes from my ear, and slowly trails down my cheek.

Cade leans forward and with the softest touch, kisses it away.

"Then came the headaches, the pains in my stomach, the constant tiredness and fatigue. By this time, I'd started university and was struggling to keep up with my studies." I continue, but now my voice is higher, strong and laced with annoyance, "I'd always been an outstanding student. I wasn't Einstein by any means, but I was up there with the best in classes. I'd worked hard, determined to follow my dream of being an interior designer, but I ended up missing so many classes that it became pointless."

"It affected you that much." Cade squeezes my hand, his comment not a question, but a clear acknowledgment of how it was for me."

"Cade, from the minute I woke up, pains would start and I would just curl up in bed and try to drift back to sleep. I tried to hide it from Mum, I didn't want her to worry, but it was only a matter of time until she noticed that something was up."

"It's clear that you and your mother are close," he whispers."

"She took me to see the doctor and they did that many scans and various tests, I was dizzy. Every each one that came back negative, which only convinced me that something was seriously wrong."

I slowly slide my hand out of his at which, at first, he gives some resilience. But when it does come free, I wrap my arms around myself to give me comfort to enable me confess the next part of my mind blowing journey.

"Then, then came the questions," I stutter, my nervous getting the better of me.

What if my emotional baggage is too much for him and he decides to walk away?

But it's a risk I have to take, because there's been enough deceit already. I need to bare all.

"Stick a needle in me any day, that's a piece of cake, but giving an honest answer to those questions, was the hardest thing I ever did." I watch him, his eyes never drifting from my face. My heart beats a little too fast, desperately hoping that I don't read any negativity in his expression.

"You see, the one thing that was drummed into me as a child was never to lie. But there was one question that really tested my honesty, the one that, even to myself, was hard to admit and understand." This time it's me that reaches out to take his hand and he gives it without hesitation.

"Cade, I didn't lie to you about being pregnant. I just didn't offer you the information in the first place. When you asked me if Viktoria was yours, I didn't lie. I told you straight out she was. So, when they asked me if I'd ever thought of harming myself or taking my own life, I didn't lie then either. I answered truthfully, I answered yes."

He moves towards me, tugging on my hand, to bring him into his embrace, but I put my palm to his chest to keep him at arm's length.

"Depression is what my diagnosis was. I didn't believe it at first, but then the doctor explained how sometimes it can show physical signs as well as emotional ones. It all started to make sense, eventually, once I'd seen a counsellor. I didn't like the medication that they gave me though, it just made me feel like I was only masking the problem." I deep sigh. "You can try and cover up and old sofa with a fancy throw as much as you like. However, underneath, it's still an old sofa," I let out a half-hearted laugh. "So, I stopped taking them. Probably not the best decision if you ask a doctor, but it was what felt right for me."

"Then something wonderful happened," I announce with a happy exhale.

I smile, a genuine smile and I catch sight of Cade's mouth when it twitches as if not sure if he should smile along with me too.

"Kat and I had been friends for years and right out of the blue, she asked me if I wanted to move to England with her. It was scary shit, but I wanted a new life." Suddenly I stop for a second when I realise I'd missed an important part of my story. "Oh yes, I forgot to tell you. Through all this, it didn't help that Michal was being a bit of a stalker, kept trying to force me to go back to him, which gave me another good reason to move. It was the best thing I could have done, Cade, because no one knew me, no one judged me and slowly I got the one thing I missed the most. I got me back." I tap my fingers against the centre of his chest to emphasize my words before shuffling backwards and putting a little more distance between us. "I did, however, make a promise to myself that no man would ever make me feel worthless to the point of self-destruction ever again. I built a barricade around myself, one where I could step out of any time I wanted, have fun, flirt, even party. But when things got too heavy, I would take a step back, slip behind my protective wall with the biggest fuck off no entry sign you can imagine. I was in control."

While listening to the last bit of my mumbled confession, Cade has slowly moved us further up the bed and is now sitting with his back against the head of the bed, his long legs stretched out in front of him. He looks downcast, and that wasn't my intention when I start my revelation.

"When I first saw you at the wedding, Cade, you were hot and way out of my league, so when you sought me out at the reception, well, I was overwhelmed."

"You didn't show it," he smirks. "In fact, you were confident and sassy. Oh, and by the way, I was the one that wasn't worthy of you, not the other way around."

"Aww give over, flatterer." I smile and I get a smile back. "The way you took care of me that night when I was pissed. That was so sweet. The day at the market, now that got me thinking, and I realised you were quite the gentleman."

"Flatterer, sweet and a gentleman. Wow! I guess I could have worse things on my resume."

"How about demolition man?" I move towards him, bringing one of my legs over his so I straddle him. "Cade, I can't be certain when or where it happened, but you've broken down the barricade."

Cade's hands go to my hips, his fingers gripping as he pulls me nearer to him. His semi-hard cock nestles between us. I go to push up on my knees so I can position myself, but he holds me firmly in place.

"What are you saying, Petra?" his lips hover over mine. "Are you telling me you want to be with me? Because I meant every word when I said I wanted us to work, that I'm willing to do whatever possible to have a legitimate relationship with you. Why do you think I agreed to work with Isaac? I was practically ready to move to Bath, to make it my base, only having to go back to New York when necessary?"

"I…"

"Also, it meant I could be with you."

"Cade, I'm sorry. I should have handled this differently, but I was scared. Scared that you were too good to be true. I should have trusted my instincts. I should have trusted you."

"I'm sorry too. I should have come after you, not taken no for an answer, but I didn't," his lips brush mine. "You're not the only one who put up barriers. I too, was reluctant to move in a different direction than what I'd perceived my life would take. But then you came along and flipped my world." He kisses me this time but only a short, sweet peck. "I think you got me the first time you called me Cowboy. Every single time I heard that word from your lips, it was like igniting a touch paper straight to my dick. No one has ever had that kind of effect on me, no one, and to be brutally honest, it was unnerving. Then I realised it wasn't that I didn't want a relationship, a family and everything that went with it. It was that I didn't want it with just anyone. I wanted it all with you."

I can't hold back any long. I surge forward, pressing my lips to his, pushing my tongue into his soft sweet warmth and kiss him with a fierceness that even surprises me. His lips push against mine with equal ferocity, his tongue playing a hot and heated dance with mine. Cade's now fully erect cock stands proudly between us, albeit restricted by the limited space. I have two choices, but one need outweighs the other. With a hand on each of his shoulders, I push against him, taking my lips from his mouth, only to place them to the right of his Adam's apple. That's where my trail begins. I pepper kisses along his shoulders, down to his pecs, stopping to give each nipple a short sharp nip with my teeth. I continue over his spectacular abs and around his belly button, until I get to the soft blond line of hair that will lead me to my ultimate goal. I need to taste him; I need to feel him. I need his cock in my mouth.

One slow and precise lick of the head is all it takes for Cade to grab hold of my hair and let out a deep guttural moan. My body instantly responds to the sexy sound of his approval, generating further wetness between my legs as my clit throbs with need. I take him into my mouth fully, as far as I can go, and suck.

"Baby," he groans out. "Fuck baby, your mouth, fuck!"

In and out, I work his cock, each time trying to take him even deeper, until I feel the head hit the back of my throat. Saliva drips from my lips as I try to control my gag reflex. When I feel him harden further, I prepare to take all that he gives, only to be pushed away, his cock releasing from my mouth with a pop.

“Come up here so I can kiss you,” he growls and I crawl up his body until we come face to face. Every kiss he delivers comes with passion. Sometimes gentle, his lips barely touching as he nips at mine with his teeth. Other times hard and with an intensity that leaves me gasping for breath.

“Get up,” he instructs as he eases me up until I’m standing on the bed in front of him, my already wet pussy right in front of his face. He looks up and gives me the filthiest of looks.

“Now it’s my turn.”

When his warm breath hits my wetness as he breathes in my essence, I shiver. When his tongue slips through the already swollen flesh, a direct hit to my clit, my legs begin to quiver.

“Fuck me, baby. I can’t get enough of your smell, your sweet taste. I want you to come for me, baby. Come on my tongue.”

His dirty words have me reeling and it only takes a few minutes under his attentive mouth before I’m coming hard. I can hardly stand, but his powerful arms keep me firmly in place as he continues to suck on my clit.

“No more,” I pant out, trying to push his head from between my legs. “Please Cade, no more.” Showing me mercy, he lowers me down and I collapse against his chest, as I try desperately to catch my breath.

Cade sweeps the hair from my face and I can feel his gaze upon me. I look up at him through a post sex haze, his beauty still shines radiantly.

“Come back with me, to Bath.” It’s meant to be a

question but comes out more like a plea.

"I've got to go back," I sigh "I can't afford to lose my job."

"I mean permanently. You, Viktoria, we can find somewhere together. A home."

"You want us to live together? Cade, I…"

"I know it's all a bit fast, but damn Petra, we wasted too much time being apart already. I want to go to sleep and wake up with you by my side. I want to know my baby girl is safe and sleeping under my roof. I don't want you to spend another single day spending half your time in one country, while our daughter is in another. I'm not the only one that's been missing out on her life. You have been too."

"I want to Cade, but it's not that easy. I can't roll up on Monday with a child that I've been hiding for over a year. What will people say?"

"I don't give a fuck what people say and neither should you. I know that you two are my life now and I'll be dammed if I'm gonna let office gossip stop me from living it. You say the barricades are down Petra, that you've let me in. Then what's stopping you from being with me?"

"Nothing," I announce with confidence. "Absolutely nothing at all." I let out an excited laugh. Jumping up, I bounce on the bed. Cade laughs along with me and my moment of madness. Out of breath, I fall on my knees in front of him. "There's one thing I need to tell you though."

"You have more secrets?"

"Only the one, and it's not really a secret, well not anymore anyway."

"What's that?" he pulls me onto his lap and I wrap my

arms around his neck, threading my fingers through his hair. I gaze upon his perfect face, his stunning blue eyes, and his lush mouth before I declare.

"I love you, Cowboy."

EPILOGUE

Two years later
Isaac and Amy's home in Bath.

Petra

It's unusually warm for the time of year, so Isaac has invited us all round, after deciding that it was perfect weather for a barbeque. I say all. Mikey is in Aspen, skiing with his mum and Axe and Nessa are MIA. Cade seems to think that the two of them are going through a hard patch and that's why they declined Isaac's offer.

I must admit, it's extremely relaxing here, laid horizontal on the sun lounger. The warmth of the sun on my face leaves me feeling extremely lethargic while I reflect on how my life has changed so much.

The last two years that Cade and I have official been

together have been eventful, to say the least. Life has a knack of throwing you a curve ball, just when you least expect it.

Who'd have believed that I was one of the miniscule percentage of women that the pill doesn't work for? Or maybe I'm just a slack bitch who missed a few. I guess we will never know 100% without going through a catalogue of tests. You would have thought that I'd learnt my lesson the first time around, making sure that we used a condom. Problem is, when Cade gets me all heated up, my brain ends up in a sex fuss and the only things on my mind is Cade's cock, Cade's fingers, Cade's mouth. I think you get my drift. And the spanking. Oh yes! Naughty little me couldn't resist being bad, if it meant that Cade would add a bit of sexual discipline to the equation. Cade is definitely the dominant one when it comes to the sex in our relationship. He can be controlling and demanding, but only at the right time, in the right place. The bedroom, the kitchen, any room possible where he can get me alone and fuck the hell out of me. But the rest of the time, he treats me as an equal. No scrap that! He treats me with the greatest respect, like I'm his everything, and he tells me every day, too.

I digress. Back to the subject.

So yes, I'm pregnant again. Working out the dates, it must have been within the first few days we were back together in Bratislava, but it took over a month after we had moved to Bath for it to register that something was amiss.

Two weeks after Cade had tracked me down, we all moved to Bath. Even my mum followed a few months later, but kept her home in Bratislava so she can make regular visits back home. Cade was adamant that she should have her own space with us, but the freedom to come and go as she pleased. He thought it was imperative that Mum continued to have the special relationship that she already had with Viktoria, to stay a constant in her life. Deep down, he held strong family views, and it was important to him that bonds between family members were strong and secure, never to be broken. He's constantly on at me about getting married. Who would have believed it from the man who used to be a bit of a commitment-phobe? Yet, it was me that was the one saying, maybe soon, what's the rush, let's discuss it later. I guess the real reason was that I was so blissfully happy with our life that it terrified me that it would jinx it.

When we first moved over, Isaac insisted we stayed with them. The news that they were an aunt and uncle for the first time, and that Sam had a cousin barely two months younger than him, came as a bit of a shock. Apparently, Kat never betrayed my trust, not really anyway, but had made it clear to Amy that it was important that Cade talked to me and sooner rather than later. Hence the call to Isaac and Cade being on the next plane to Bratislava.

Within minutes, the room was full of hugs, back slapping and celebrations. However, Isaac took great joy in getting his revenge by constantly being on Cade's back, passing remarks about being tied down. I think his words were, who's the one that's pussy whipped now?

It didn't take us long to find somewhere big enough for us all. In fact, the house had an annex off to the side which was perfect for Mum. We had two guest rooms too, so we were even graced with a visit from Ben, who came to stay for a couple of weeks to help us get the house in shape.

It was when Ben stayed, I realised I'd missed my period. At first, I'd try to tell myself that it was just the stress of moving and everything, but deep down I knew. While Cade was out with Ben, picking up paint and Viktoria was having a nap, I took a test. I was scared shitless. Cade was going to go ape shit. A baby? So soon? To make sure, I took another, then another. Three tests later, all showing up positive, my head was all over the place.

As Cade and Ben walked in, I mumbled something about having to go get milk. Grabbing the car keys out of Cade's hand, not even a pause for a kiss, I made a beeline for the door. I drove to the one place I knew I could vent.

When Kat opened the door, she had found me stood on her doorstep a blubbering mess. I spluttered out my predicament as she guided me into her apartment and onto the sofa.

She listened as I ranted through my tears and sobs, voicing my worries about how Cade was going to react and how this surely would ruin our unconventional, fledgling relationship. Kat, being Kat, told me to get a grip, go home and tell him. She then, in the nicest possible way, reminded me I'd already kept too much information from him and that this time, good or bad, he deserved to know.

I sat outside the house for what seemed like ages, playing out every possible scenario in my head, each one seeming to end up with me losing everything. I was sick to the stomach with trepidation. When I plucked up enough courage to step out of the car, I stormed into the house with a do or die attitude. My temporary bravery dispersed immediately when I'd entered the kitchen and found Cade sat on one of the high stools at the counter, tapping away on his laptop. His gaze immediately met mine. A soft smile played upon his lips; his eyes full of adoration.

"I'm pregnant," I had blurted out, my body shaking in fear, my heart in my mouth, waiting for his reaction.

"Really?" he had said, jumping off the stool and storming towards me. Picking me up, he'd spun me around before taking my breath away with his hard, heated kisses. "Damn, baby. That's the best fucking thing, just the best." When I burst into tears, he held me tight. "Hey, what's wrong? Are you okay, is the baby okay? Petra, baby, you're scaring me."

"I was scared. I wasn't sure you would want this. It's so soon."

"Baby, I love you. Of course, I want this," he had replied. "It's fucking awesome. You know both you and Viktoria are my life, and nothing will ever change that. But this time, I get to see you carry my child and watch you bloom and grow. I can't wait to see our baby being born. Hold them from the very first moment, be there from the very start. You are giving me a second chance, and I can't thank you enough." His love making that night was gentle, caring and full of emotion. We held each other for so long afterwards, as we shared tears of love and joy. Cade is not a crier, so I knew that this was something monumentally special for him. For us.

We had a few prenatal scares, which meant Cade fell into the role of overprotective baby daddy, putting me on bedrest and a sex ban. He was pretty rubbish at it, because hell, I was having none of it. Although I would never put our baby at risk, I knew he was just being overcautious. Anyhow, this time during pregnancy, I was horny all the fricking time and it sure as hell didn't help that Cade was in such close proximity. I couldn't keep my hands off him. Eventually, he gave in to me, and for those few months, I was totally in control. He said that he preferred it that way, as I knew exactly what my limits were while pregnant. He also told me not to get used to it, because after the baby, it would be business as usual. I couldn't wait.

Cade still has to fly back to Miami now and then, but it's becoming less and less since he took the position working with Isaac. He would never let go of his company and continues to keep a close eye on it, but he has an excellent team in place, who he trusts implicitly. This option of taking a back seat works perfectly, only having to attend monthly meetings, some of those via video link.

I no longer work for Isaac. Although, in general, everyone was great when the news got out about Cade and me, I still found it too uncomfortable to stay. I felt guilty about not earning any money to bring into the household, but Cade supported me 100%, and besides, I got to spend quality time with Viktoria before the new baby arrived.

However, when Cade suggested I should find something of interest to me, something just for myself, I brushed it off as being ridiculous. But the more I thought about it, the more it made sense. It wasn't going to be easy, but I resurrected my dream of being an interior designer. I checked courses and what options I had, working out if it would be possible without jeopardising too much time with my family. When

I voiced my thoughts and ideas with my mum, she was full of excitement, telling me she would support me all the way. Cade was absolutely over the moon when I laid out my plans. He was so supportive that in my hormonal state; I ended up a complete mess of emotions.

So, three months after the baby was born, I started a one-year foundation diploma in art and design, with a plan to do a degree. I still feel like I've missed out on the total university experience, but I still had good enough qualifications to get accepted. If I work hard, I'm confident that I will accomplish my goal.

Even before I had any design qualification under my belt, Isaac had me seconded as an adviser when Amy decided that the Bath offices needed a complete overall. I was nervous at first, as hotel rooms were my niche thing, but once I'd got involved, it was a breeze.

My life has come full circle. From being a depressed and mixed-up girl who escaped to a new life, with an outer shell that gave the impression of a confident, flirtatious woman, yet with less than a handful of friends. I had fooled myself into thinking that I was happy having control over my life, protected by the invisible walls that I had erected. Only now realising that I can only truly be free from those restraints. Cade has done that for me. He has broken down that barricade, held me so I didn't fall and has given me the strength to be my true self.

Will I ever trust, honour and obey?

I trust him implicitly.

I'm honoured to be showered with his love.

I will obey him always… in the bedroom!

Cade

"We need more drinks," Amy announces, walking in from the backyard, thrusting a large glass pitcher into my unexpected hands.

"And you want me to make it?" I ask, only taking hold before it slips to the floor.

"You make the best margaritas." Her smile is sweet, full of shiny white teeth and exaggerated, as is the flutter of her eyelashes. I shake my head at her and laugh. I can never say no to her.

"Yes ma'am," I stand up straight, click my heels, and salute her. At which she simply tuts and walks away.

My eyes fall on Petra, laid out on one of the loungers. Her shorts have risen up, and I'm sure I can see the edge of her bright pink panties right at the apex of her legs. My dick twitches and I have to fight the urge to go out there and disgrace myself in front of the family. "Damn!" I mutter before forcing myself to turn away.

I rinse the pitcher under the cold water, fill it with ice, and start to mix the margarita.

When it had come to choosing between my life in Miami or being with Petra and Viktoria, I didn't even have to consider it. It was a done deal. I'd already been willing to move over to Bath to work for Isaac, if it meant that I could pursue a relationship with Petra. Sure, things went a little faster than expected, but when I found out I was going to be a dad again, this time having the chance to be a part of it all, I had to keep my emotions in check. At least until I had a private moment. That moment was with Petra, and when we shared it, it reinforced our commitment to each other even more.

After the news of the pregnancy, while Ben was still staying with us, my parents flew over from Florida. Ben and my parents knew nothing of Viktoria, well it's not something you drop on someone in a telephone call. With Ben arriving to stay with us, of course, we introduced him to his niece. However, I swore him to secrecy as it was only right that Mum and Dad heard it from me. For once, he kept his big mouth shut. So, when my parents arrived, let's just say it was a tough time.

When we sat them down and told them about Viktoria, all hell let loose. My parents have always been heavily involved with the church, but my dad's reactions were anything but charitable. My mother just sat, shoulders slumped and cried as my dad raged, spouting words that immediately got my back up. He accused Petra of trapping me, only after my money, the exact fears that had consumed Petra, the reason she'd kept her secret.

I lost it, I absolutely lost it. Don't get me wrong, I've had my spats with my father before, but this time, I raged. I was like a man possessed. I demanded, how dare he speak about Petra like that, the woman that I was in love with? It got extremely heated. My mother's uncharacteristic high-pitched screaming, telling us to shut up, was enough to shock us out of our disagreement. My father stormed out of the front door that he'd not long since arrived through. I was ready to follow him, demand that he apologised to Petra and make him realise that whatever his illogical ideas he had about her, she was the mother of his grandchild. But then Petra had put her hand out to stop me. I watch with a mixture of apprehension and admiration when she was the one who went to fight our case.

I still don't know to this day what Petra said to my dad, but after an agonising thirty minutes, they both walked back in. My dad's arm draped around her waist, talking as if they were old acquaintances.

All it took was one look, one single moment spent with Viktoria, and they were besotted with her.

Fortunately, when we announced the surprise news of another grandchild, it was met with cries of great joy.

Which leads me to Kristina.

Watching Petra go through the birth of our second daughter had me ready to punch something. Seeing her in such pain and not being able to do anything to help her was as painful as a shot to the balls. When the nurse laid that perfect little girl in my arms, I was crying like a baby, not giving a damn who was watching. It was like I'd been blessed with another angel, bringing my total to three.

The squeal of a child's laugh brings me out of my daydream and I steady my stance, just in time for Sam and Viktoria to collide with my legs. Arms wrapped tight as one clings on the left, and the other clings to the right. Their giggles are intermittent while they try to catch their breaths. Kristina, and Isaac and Amy's daughter Ruby, are both down for a nap, but even these noisy two, couldn't wake them as they are both heavy sleepers.

"Hey, you two, what are you doing?"

"We're playing kiss catch, silly. Aunt Amy told us how to play it?" Viktoria explains with a serious face. "Don't pretend you don't know how to play Daddy; I've seen you playing it with Mummy."

"Yeah, but Mummy and Daddy are adults," I say as I grab the pitcher and start walking out towards the back. It's a slow and tiresome process, with the weight of a four-year-old on each leg. Maybe I should increase the reps at the gym next week. "Aunt Amy is naughty, because you're not allowed to play that game until you're… twenty-one." Viktoria giggles and I realise having girls will not be easy.

When I step out into the yard, the kids detach themselves and go running off towards the play gym over to the far side. I ditch the pitcher, but not before I've scooped out a chuck of ice with the large mixer spoon. I move over to where Petra is still laid, I stand at her side, blocking the sun. The loss of heat is enough to have her shielding her eyes and lifting her gaze up at me.

"Cade?" I stand looking at her, taking time to gaze upon her beauty. "Cade, what's up?" I hunker down at the side of her and she makes to sit up. I put my hand on her ankle to stop her. She jumps when the cold ice hits her sun kissed skin. She shivers when I slowly run it up the inside of her leg. I move nearer, so my body shields what I'm doing to her from the view of others. When I hit the apex of her legs, I push the smaller piece of ice under the edge of her shorts and panties until I touch soft flesh. She hisses as the coldness hits her clit. Her head falls back, her eyelids drop to almost closed as I stroke her with my icy fingers. When she starts to moan, I cover her mouth with mine to silence her. I remove my hand and capture the whimper of disappointment with a deeper, harder kiss. I stand to move away from her.

"Cade, what was that all about?" she questions.

"A taste of what's coming tonight," I say with all seriousness. I hold out my hand. She takes it and I pull her to her feet.

"Woah, Cowboy," she gives me a sultry look. "Is that a promise?"

"No baby, that's an order." I lean over and brush my lips against her ear before nipping it with my teeth. "I'm going to do all kinds of dirty things to you until you can't take anymore. You will scream for me to stop, but I won't. Not until you submit and give me the one thing I need," I whisper.

"And what is it that I need to submit to?" she asks breathlessly.

"Marry me."

***

Amy

"It's about bloody time," I grumble while talking to Isaac's reflection in the mirror that sits above the bathroom basin. "I thought he would never pop the question." I put my toothbrush back in the holder and dry my face with a small hand towel. Everyone had left a couple of hours ago, so when Cade had phoned to speak to Isaac while we were putting the kids to bed, I was a little concerned that something was up.

"You can't blame Cade." He sniggers and I can feel the heat radiate from Isaac's body when he stands close behind me. "He's been asking her to marry him for months."

With his hands resting on each side of me on the counter, he's actually not touching me, but the way my body reacts to his closeness, he might as well be. I temporary lose my track of thought, but then suddenly remember what we were discussing.

"Really?" I gasp. "That surprises me. She said nothing. He must have done something special to finally get her to agree."

"I'm damn sure he did," he winks at me in the reflection. Bending a little, he nibbles my ear and I know exactly what's coming next. Yep. There you go. One hand cups my right breast, the other slides between my legs as he pushes his hard cock between my arse cheeks. "I fucking love your tits," he growls. He's insatiable.

Even though I'm still in my underwear, it doesn't put Isaac off in the slightest and to be honest, his touch has the same arousing effect on me as if I was stark bollock naked.

Moving his hand from my right breast to my left, he slides it under the cup of my bra and scissors my nipple between two fingers. His other hand is quite busy, having already slipped past the waistband of my knickers. With his talented hands, the dirty words he whispers and the nip of his teeth at my neck, I come; right there, pressed against the sink unit. God, he's good!

"Turn around, I need to fuck you."

"Not so fast." I hit back as I duck under his arm, even

with orgasm induced jelly legs. He quickly turns, so he's facing me with his back against the basin. Before he has time to make a move, I lean forward and take his nipple into my mouth. He lets out a groan, his hands gripping hard on the edge of the unit, his chest pushed forward eager for more contact. After nipping and sucking until his little nips are like sherbet pips, I follow the outline of his tattoo with my tongue. His breathing becomes more and more erratic when I work down to his zipper line that vanishes into his Calvin Klein boxers. Hooking my thumbs into the waistband at each side, I look up at him while I drag them down and over his hips.

"By the way," I give him a sultry smile. "Why didn't you tell me that Axe and Nessa are having relationship problems?"

"Baby, leave it," he pants out as his cock bounces out of the fabric. "Don't get involved."

"Why not?" I lick the bead of cum that's resting on the tip. "Look how well it turned out with Petra and Cade. I'm sure we can help them sort it out."

"Amy, no." he's trying his best to sound demanding, but with my tongue sliding up his shaft, he's like putty in my hands. Soon to be in my mouth. "Axe and Nessa's relationship is complicated. There are things from their past that Axe… Amy, stay out of it."

"Maybe I'll invite Nessa to lunch," I suck hard, taking him in right to the back of my throat. His hand comes to my head and grabs a hand full of hair. I slowly slide him back out of my mouth until only the tip is past my lips. My words are a little mumbled as I talk around his cock. "I've been meaning to ask her for ages how they met."

"Woman!" he hisses.

"Sorry, baby, can't talk now. I've kind of got my mouthful."

The End

ACKNOWLEDGMENTS

This book was originally released as Breaking Down the Barricade, Reed and Rice Series. Four years later I decided that it needed a facelift. So now with a new name, Taking A Chance, new sexy cover and a bloody good edit, it's all shiny and new.

No author can do without the fabulous people that are their invisible scaffolding. So, I would like to give them a shout out and uber huge thank you.

My good friends and book loving queens, Jackie McLeish, Nikki Young and Lynn Scott. Extra shout out for Nikki for her hard work in looking after the reader group and casting the first eye over my WIP's.

Big thankyou to Lou at LJ Design and Caroline Stainburn for your excellent work. Without your expertise this book would be one hell of a shit show.

A special thank you to my pimpets and beta readers: Kirsty Adams, Helen Simpson, Victoria Philpott, Ann Walker, Joanne Edmunds, Lesley Robson, Nikki Robertson, Sarah Van Aker, Sophie Richards, Yvonne Eason and Wendy Susan Hodges. You all rock.

KL Shandwick, Ava Manello, Tracie Podger, The Indie Girls and all my author friends for their support and many words of wisdom.

My reader group - T.L Wainwrights All Things Naughty Reader Group. Thank you for the feedback and support you have given me. Love you guys!

My family and friends both in and out of the book world.

ALSO AVAILABLE BY T.L WAINWRIGHT

Young Outlaws MC Series

Unlawful –book 1.

Justice - book 2.

Vengeance – book 3

Damaged Alpha Series

DEACON. Soldier. Fighter – book 1

TOMEK Saving angels – book 2

CHARLIE If only – book 3

JORDAN Broken Promise – book 4

Reed & Rice Series

Catching A Breath

Taking A Chance

Standalones

Dream F*#k's And Hard Drives

A Hole Lotto Loving

My Sweet Gi

Play for Me

That Man Sam

ABOUT THE AUTHOR

I'm T.L Wainwright and live in Leeds, Yorkshire, England . Working full-time in the Freight industry since leaving school I found that I my downtime was wasted. That is until I found writing.

I wrote my first book back in 2015 and since then, my life had been one big delightful experience. It's never and won't ever be about the money, it's simply all about the storytelling.

I can only hope that my words are entertaining and at the very least put a smile on your face.

YOU CAN FIND T.L HERE:

facebook.com/tlwainwright

Twitter: @wainwright_tl

Instagram: wainwright.tl

bookbub.com/authors/t-l-wainwright

goodreads.com/author/show/14162871.T_L_Wainwright

T.L
Wainwright
The Naughty One

Printed in Great Britain
by Amazon

69933418R00127